PET TALES

by Rachel Gies

Copyright © 2020 by
Fairburn Publishing

No part of this book may be reproduced in any format without the written consent of the author.

Pet Tales is a work of fact & fiction. The people, events, and places that figure into the stories are products of the author's imagination or are used fictitiously. Any resemblance to actual events, locales, or persons, living or dead, is coincidental. Except her family and pet stories.

Thank you Joy Shrout for reading my original manuscripts and preparing them for the newspaper.

Proofreading/Editing: Molly Eaton
Cover Photos submitted by friends of the Waupaca Humane Society and family.

ISBN: 978-0-9709960-4-6

pottsinwisco@yahoo.com

"Nittany" painted by Pearl Meiers

The awesome cover for *Pet Tales* was made possible thanks to Monica Gardner of the Waupaca Humane Society who shared our callout for pet photos on the Humane Society FB page and got 4,385 peoples' attention making us viral!

Please see contributing pet's names on the *Dedication* page following. We are so grateful and hope to sell our dog treats at the Farmer's Market soon to raise more dough for our favorite furrever friends at the Waupaca Humane Society. *See our recipe in the back of this book.*

Rachel and her granddog, Payton

    This book was so much fun with all of the help we received. I love writing about animals. They are all such characters. This book contains stories passed on from my family back in Amsterdam to my immediate family's pet stories and a couple tales from young student writers who wrote stories just for this book.

    I am so honored to have such great photos of Humane Society rescues for the cover as well as the young illustrators who brought these stories to life with their pictures! The work that went into it by all of these kids impresses and inspires me—Thank you all! For those who enjoy a little pet tale I hope you enjoy this book as much as we enjoyed making it.

Rachel

Dedication

I would like to dedicate *Pet Tales* to my six grand-critters;
Scott, Ryan, Lauren, Danny, Braxton and Breanna.

Special thanks to our beloved cover pets:

Teddy & Titan	Liv
Vesper	Taz
Kirby formerly known as Morris	Beth
Thor	Tucker
Red	Sadie the Adventure Pup
Bella	Link
PhoeBe	Lunchbox
Kitty (the Rottweiler)	Cash
Makani	Chief
Kyra	B.J. Raji
Koy	Carlos
Becca	Patches
Lux & Liv	Tank & Junior
Ahmie	Skrunch
Lexi	Chooch
Travis	Shelby
Deke	Ashby
Ash	Schermetzler Pup
Seeger & Teal	Lenz Pup
Sasha	Gallegos Pets
Rusty	Cairo
Mikka	Ferra
Chloe	Shmeegs
Sleeping Bella	Dora
Scarlett	Googi
Spot	Zoe
Barbie & Frank	Kodiak
Dougie	Biscuit :)

When Rachel approached me to work on another book with her I jumped at the chance. We had so much fun with *Foxy Tale, One Size Fits Most, Captured Pearl and the Darkness Within*. Rachel is so creative and loves new ideas, animals, and kids. Putting this book together for her was an honor.

Working with 4th-7th grade kids I asked her if she would be willing to give them an opportunity to help with her book. She agreed to see if they'd like to illustrate some of her short stories. The kids loved the idea and we have collected a great deal of illustrations and a couple of stories that were actually written by students.

These kids are known in Waupaca, WI as the Wisconsin Secret Service (est. 2013). We volunteer community service and random acts of kindness. We've had global and local projects and we take care of our four-legged friends and fellow students as well as our teachers with donations or inspirational surprises. For *Pet Tales* we got together and made our own sketch books and kids picked from fifty short stories to illustrate. COVID19 made planning and getting together so uncertain and virtual schooling put new pressures on our kids working from home. Not being able to get together, they still loved to help. Rachel even let the kids vote on who to share her proceeds with and they agreed unanimously to help the children at Saint Jude's Children's Hospital. Rachel also surprised us by letting the kids have 200 books to sell themselves and use the money for future projects.

Thank you for purchasing this book. Cover photos were donated by Facebook fans who have adopted dogs from the Humane Society. Our healthy dog treat recipe is in the back of this book. We make, bake, bag and tag at the Middle School with six ovens at once. Proceeds always go to the Humane Society.

Camin Potts
Fine Print Graphic Design
Waupaca, Wisconsin Secret Service (on FB and YouTube)

Table of Contents

CHAPTER 1:	BRINGING HOME A PET	9
CHAPTER 2:	LUCKY MONKEY	13
CHAPTER 3:	PIETEKA	16
CHAPTER 4:	MY LITTLE BUDDY	19
CHAPTER 5:	SHOELESS	22
CHAPTER 6:	WHAT A PIG	24
CHAPTER 7:	WHAT LURKS BELOW	27
CHAPTER 8:	SMITTY THE KITTY	30
CHAPTER 9:	MY BEST FRIENDS CHARLIE AND CHUCKIE	33
CHAPTER 10:	TRAINING HENRY	36
CHAPTER 11:	YODA AND GIUSEPPE	39
CHAPTER 12:	SHARING LADDIE	43
CHAPTER 13:	BOOGIE AND BART	45
CHAPTER 14:	GLASS KISSES	49
CHAPTER 15:	VET TO GO	51
CHAPTER 16:	A HOME FOR MAC	55
CHAPTER 17:	SPARKY	59

CHAPTER 18:	WHEN WE LOSE A BELOVED PET	61
CHAPTER 19:	GOIN' ON A GUILT TRIP	65
CHAPTER 20:	CAT BATH	69
CHAPTER 21:	STRAY CATS	73
CHAPTER 22:	BUNNIES IN THE BASEMENT	77
CHAPTER 23:	UNEXPECTED FRIEND	83
CHAPTER 24:	FLY IN THE CAT BOX	85
CHAPTER 25:	PAMPERED PETS	89
CHAPTER 26:	COCO AND CHANEL	93
CHAPTER 27:	MOUSE CATCHERS	96
CHAPTER 28:	LOST AND FOUND	99
CHAPTER 29:	DEAR LITTLE FELLA	101
CHAPTER 30:	THE GIFT	103
CHAPTER 31:	A GOATEE TALE	107
CHAPTER 32:	THE TALE OF FRED	109
SECRET SERVICE HEALTHY STEALTHY PET TREAT RECIPE		111

Chapter 1

BRINGING HOME A PET

Its happened to many soft hearted animal lovers. You're at the pet store and see the cutest little kitten with the cutest little paws and great big eyes, just begging for your attention. Or maybe your eyes focus on a darling miniature poodle whose stubby little tail seems to be wagging just for you. Maybe its a chameleon, fish, hamster, chinchilla, parrot, hedgehog, WHATEVER! Next thing you know, you're loading up on pet food. If you're like most of us, falling in love with a pet is easy. And it's no wonder! Sharing your home with a four-legged friend is one of life's greatest joys. They give us unconditional love, loyalty and acceptance. Suddenly you're not alone in the world. You have someone to come home to, something that relies on you and shows their appreciation in a lick or a tail wag.

When considering adopting a pet, it is a big decision that requires plenty of thought and preparation due to the care they need and what you can afford. Deciding who will take Pluto out is important before you bring him home. They require lots of time, money, and commitment. Too often people get caught up in the excitement and "fun times" of owning a dog and neglect to think about all that goes with them. Feeding a dog and taking them out for a late night walk is vital to their health and happiness. Once you've made the decision to take in a pet you're responsible for its care for the rest of their life.

PET TALES By Rachel Gies

It's sad that many people don't take this all into consideration before they get a pet. Adopting a pet just because it's cute, you feel sorry for it, or because the kids have been whining for a puppy can be a big mistake you can't really take back. Don't forget that pets may be with you 10, 15, even 20 years. They require food, water, exercise, care, and companionship everyday. Its also important to consider the cost of pet ownership because it can add up quick. Think about having to buy licenses, and the cost of spaying and neutering, veterinary care, grooming, toys, food, kitty litter, flea infestations, scratched up furniture, chewed up shoes, so many "accidents" house training, unexpected medical emergencies are all unfortunate but common aspects of pet ownership.

Consider also that many rental communities don't allow pets and the cost of daycare and boarding adds to daily expenses and vacation costs. If you have kids under six years old you might consider waiting a few years before you adopt a pet. Small children often aren't mature enough to be responsible for their pets.

Some dogs mature well after 3 years of age. When potty training, puppies need to be taken outside right after eating, drinking and naps and many times in between. It really takes a lot of patience training a puppy. Cats, however, require little training. Just show them where the litter box is and they get it. They enjoy being left alone, they don't need nightly walks and are great company when they want to be.

Before adopting a pet, do some research on how much time you need to spend each day training and caring for it. That way, you'll ensure you choose an animal that will fit your lifestyle and your living arrangements. Also, when you do a lot of traveling, you'll need either reliable friends and neighbors or money to pay for boarding or pet-sitting service.

Having your pet spayed or neutered, obeying community leash and licensing laws, and keeping identification tags and chips on your pets are all part of being a responsible owner. Of course, giving your pet love, companionship, exercise, a healthy diet, and regular veterinary care are essentials. When you adopt a pet, you make a commitment to care for the animal for his or her entire lifetime. Pets provide us with unconditional love. Let's give them ours. ✱

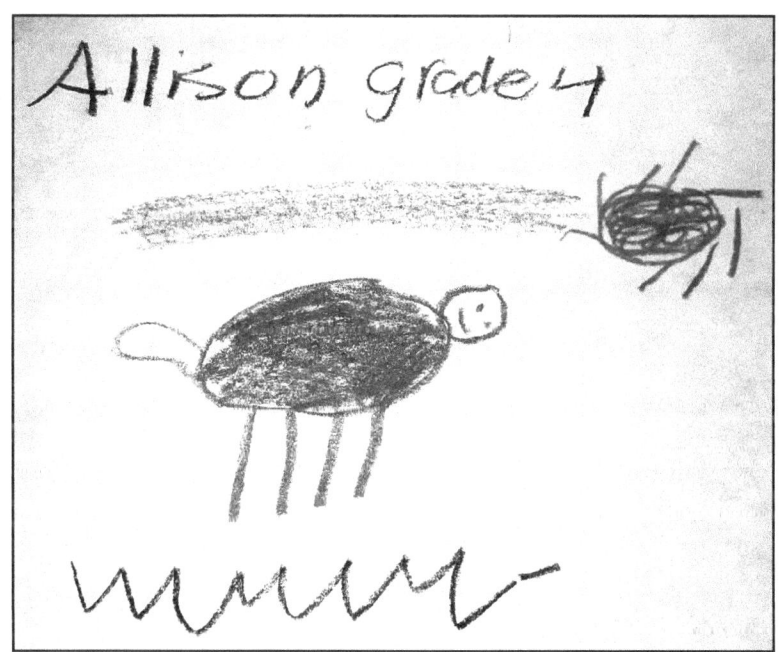

Chapter 2

LUCKY MONKEY

I was thinking about all of the pets I've owned from kid to adult and the kind of pets I've never had. My idea of a pet is something furry, cute and cuddly, that you can play with and maybe even teach some tricks. I can't imagine ever owning a scorpion, tarantula or any dessert creature. Snakes, and lizards are a big No for me. When it comes to scaled things fish are as far as I'll go, and I love fish.

What makes it so exciting to have these creatures as a pet? If thats what you like, then I admire you. Everyone should be loved as much as a dog or a cat. I'm sure they are easy to care for but what can you do with them besides stare at them and sprinkle a daily dose of creeping/crawling food? And what if they climb out of their habitat and start roaming the house? Wouldn't that be dangerous? I have to be able to hold my pet and I'm not picking that up! But that's just me.

I've loved a lot of pets and I've had plenty of them over the years. One of the most unusual pets I had ever been around was a monkey. When I was a child, one of my neighbors brought home a monkey. This was a long time ago in Amsterdam where the weird and unusual creatures were accepted more easily. My neighbor, who had traveled a great deal, was known for picking up all that is strange and unusual. His wife thought he went too far when he brought home this monkey! Eventually, she too fell in love with the little guy. He named the monkey Jocko. He was so petite and stood

PET TALES By Rachel Gies

about ten inches in length with a tail just as long and tiny hands and feet. He was so small he looked fragile. But you couldn't let that fool you. Jocko seemed to have the strength of a gorilla when he needed to. Once at the outdoor market he grabbed a banana off a cart and no one could get it away from him. He made it clear that it was time to purchase the yellow fruit.

My neighbor was one of my favorite people, he had a flair for unique things. He and his wife owned snakes, a tarantula, several exotic birds, canaries, geese and ducks. It was a zoo of an odd collections. Rain Forest meets desert meets farm. God only knew what he would bring home next.

Once in a while he would ask us to babysit for his zoo of misfits or bring a critter by to watch for him. He would say that he would come by and pick it up later. Well, later didn't exactly happen when it came to Jocko the monkey. Our neighbor assured us that he would come for Jocko just as soon as he built an additional room for him. However, this project would take forever as we found out later. So, Jocko became part of our family for a while.

Jocko was always the center of attention while he stayed with us. He learned early-on to get the attention he wanted by entertaining everyone. He'd show off his talents with all kinds tricks. I think if we would have taken him on the road or if he joined the circus he would have made a small fortune. He was amazing. He learned to dance, somersault, do cartwheels, shake hands with men and kiss women on the cheek. He would perform only when he knew a treat awaited him. Jocko would smile after he'd receive his reward and when it was time to retire for the night he would slip inside his small decorative cage and sleep until sunrise.

Jocko was used to living in a warm, tropical climate year round. The poor thing couldn't acclimate to the cold and bitter winter weather of the Netherlands and keeping him in a cage went against his very

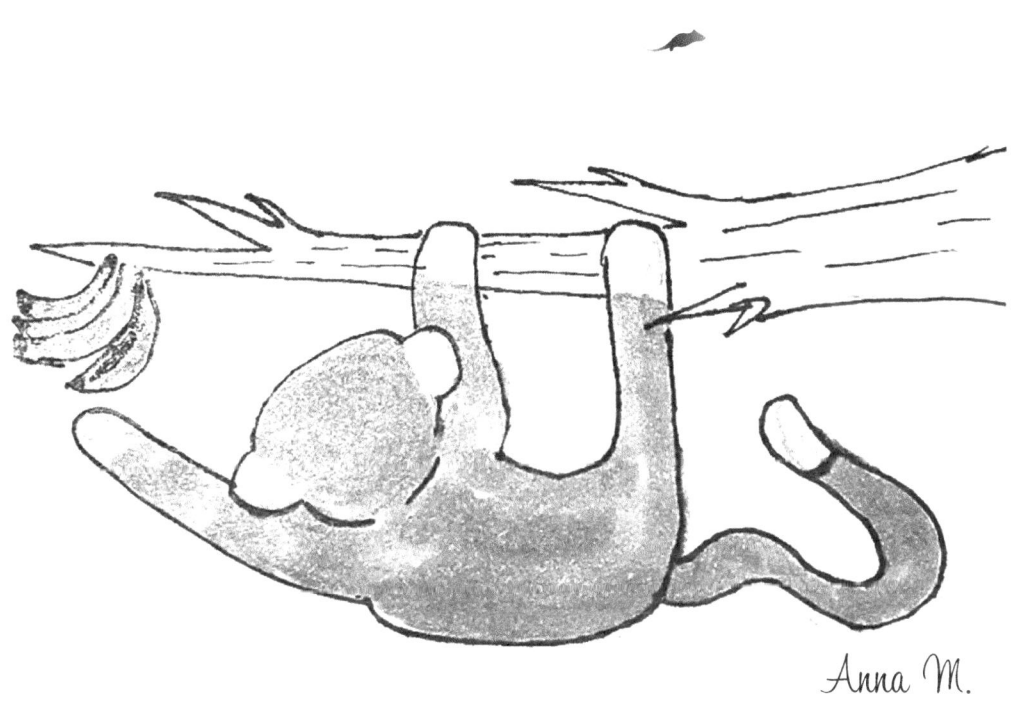

Anna M.

nature. Within a year, it was clear that poor Jocko was becoming ill. My mom knitted him blankets and little sweaters for him to wear. We all realized, that Jocko didn't belong there. Fortunately, there was a local zoo nearby, and with our neighbor's permission, we took Jocko there. He received immediate care. At first we were heart-broken, giving up our little buddy who had become one of the family, but we knew he was better off.

    Jocko enjoyed his life at the zoo. He met his girlfriend, Clara, another monkey who flirted with him shamelessly. They became inseparable. She'd hold Jocko in her hairy arms close to her bosom and rock him to sleep. He and Clara had several little monkey babies and ended up spending many happy years together behind bars. *

Chapter 3

PIETEKA

Oh, the stories I could share about Pieteka could fill a book. Pieteka was a smart beaked Mynah bird who had come into our life and stole my mother's heart. This was quite by accident because no way would my mom keep an animal let alone a Mynah bird that pooped the cage and spewed his rage. He was, however, mom's favorite after she took him in when he was left on her doorstep. No one minded at first but it soon became obvious that this creature was a pain in the tuckus; in Yiddish "tuckus" means "butt". Pieteka would wake up and screech loudly until someone removed the shawl from atop his cage. It was worse than an alarm clock but everyone learned to wake up early before the bird.

Mom adored the creature and to this day no one in the family could understand why. Maybe it was because the sound coming out of its beak was just like mom's voice. She couldn't leave Pieteka home alone, so he accompanied her to the coffee shop every day since I was little. He was beautiful, so colorful and seemingly happy, flitting around in his cage. But he was messy, sassy and he'd poop nonstop. Mom would scrub the cage first thing in the morning but by noon it looked like a cow swept through dropping pies and boy it stank so bad. Maybe she should have changed his bird seed? Dad always threatened to stuff him and cook him up for supper.

It was clear that we were never to criticize the little monster because Pieteka was Mom's favorite. The rest of the family, Dad included, took a back seat in mom's life. Mynah birds can live a very long time and Pieteka lived to the ripe old age of eighteen years but a few locals wished for his early demise. A few customers actually enjoyed the little guy's crazy antics but not many.

Occasionally a customer would demand quick service or complain about the food. Pieteka would screech at them, fluent in Dutch, Russian or Hungarian, depending on who he learned the insults from. Customers would chuckle at his language and enjoy the cut downs, however, a few realized that he learned to talk like that from mom and they were very insulted to hear how she referred to her customers. Pieteka even mimicked the sound of her voice to perfection.

I remember an incident when my Uncle, Pastor George and his wife, Aunt Alice, came to visit us for a few days from Norway and it turned into a disaster. Aunt Alice thought she heard my mom insulting her behind her back. She was so upset she fainted and hit her head on the coffee table. She required nineteen stitches across her forehead. Of course, it was Pieteka.

The bird was put in the bedroom for the rest of their visit because Mom didn't want him cussing in front of (or behind) her sister and brother-in-law until she explained the situation with the naughty mimicker. Once introduced to Pieteka they understood. It was a good thing Alice and Pastor George were forgiving souls. They all had a good laugh about it, including Pieteka. Everyone agreed to be careful how they spoke around the bird. After all, you don't want anyone saying, "a little birdie told me" when that bird was Pieteka! *

My Little Buddy
Illustrated by
Cole Brotzman

Chapter 4

MY LITTLE BUDDY

It was raining cats and dogs. Buckets of water dumped from the sky. On this particular day the storm made it impossible for people to get to work because of the thunder and lightening with the torrential downpour. It was expected to rain all morning but clear up late afternoon but it didn't look like it would ever be sunny again. If you had to call in late, might as well call in sick and just stay in bed.

It was so quiet in the little coffee shop in the middle of the city of Amsterdam, but still, Mom filled up the gigantic coffee maker with fresh ground beans. The super sized pot brewed 70 cups of coffee.

Sitting inside the toasty shop watching the storm out the window and listening to the rain on the tin roof our beloved cat Mimi snuggled into my lap as she purred a soft steady tune. School happened to be closed due to a holiday and so kids would be home all day driving their stranded parents insane. As the rain began to let up and the sky lightened up to blue again the day slowly turned back to normal. People emerged to get busy with everyday life with the exception of a few locals who would sit around for hours sipping their cups of coffee and catching up on the latest gossip.

PET TALES By Rachel Gies

The door to our shop began to swing open more frequently as the weather improved and clients returned for rich coffee and fresh pastries. Mom baked tasteful little treats that hooked many of her customers who came back often to satisfy their cravings. By lunchtime Mom was off to the races preparing sandwiches as usual and way too busy to notice the little street urchin who walking in cradling a small box. As the boy came closer I craned my neck for a look into the box. I saw fur and heard a quiet whimper coming from the balls crouched in the corner. My heart melted as I saw two tiny puppies huddled together cold, wet and shaking.

Reaching inside the box I picked up both tiny creatures and they nuzzled into my neck making me giggle. The kid, who looked no more than 8 years old said, "You can have em 'cause my ma says I can't keep em." A customer and I said in unison, "I'll take one!" He only asked for fifty cents per puppy. I gladly gave the boy fifty cents of my allowance.

Mom came out holding a ladle for soup in her hand. She stopped in her tracks when she saw the puppy. "No dogs allowed". I showed her the little face. It worked! She sighed and said "okay, but the dog can't stay in the shop". Memories of Pieteka made us both shudder but helped me understand. I accepted her

Chapter 5

SHOE LESS

This story was passed down from my Dutch grandmother, Oma:

When I was a child we would always put our shoes outside the front door before going inside the house. One morning, getting ready for school, our shoes were gone! We looked everywhere—We had to pick another pair and told ourselves we would find them when we returned from school. We searched the house but no shoes could be found so we asked the neighbors if they've seen our shoes and found out it wasn't just happening to us. Everyone left their shoes outside their door and just about *everybody* was missing a shoe or two.

This was in a very tiny village in Holland and pretty much everyone was related. They'd help any of their neighbors in need but now friends turned against each other and no one trusted anyone.

Most figured it was a prank by kids but all of the kids swore their innocence and we started to feel a bit uncomfortable with the mysterious disappearance of dozens of shoes, not necessarily in pairs. Perhaps there was a burglar among us with a shoe fetish? Or some gypsy was selling them in the next town over? Days passed and neighbors continued to suspect each other. If this was a prank it had gone on too long.

At the edge of town lived Mrs. Ava White, a blind, elderly widow who lived alone, confined to a wheelchair. Villagers took turns bringing Ava to town and helped with grocery shopping while others cut her grass, brought

rule and took my little buddy upstairs for a bath. You'd never believe how clean and fluffy, Buddy (which I decided to name him) was after a bath.

We loved Buddy dearly and he loved us back. He was with us for the next fourteen years until dad decided we were moving to America. As much as we loved him we couldn't bring him with us because he was too old and too sick to travel. We spent days crying and mourned the loss of our devoted companion but were told Buddy was a happy camper at my cousins and they gave him a loving home.

Buddy got along great with their boxer, Max, and Penny, their foxy little cat. They actually fell in love with each other and made a great pet family.

I used to send letters and postcards to Buddy letting him know I loved him. My cousin Ava wrote back letting me know that he lived a very happy life until the day he died peacefully lying next to his furry family Max and Penny. He was almost 16 years old. Lucky dog had two good lives and I imagine now is living happily ever after in puppy heaven. I am sure of it. ✻

her meals, anything she needed. Ava had lived in the village longer than anyone. Bart, Ava's next door neighbor, took care of Ava more than anyone making sure she was safe and sound.

One afternoon Bart knocked on Ava's door and her dog Mack ran to greet him as he always did. Mack adored Bart because when he came over he would feed Mack and take him for walks. Mack was a huge, beautiful shepherd that was as gentle as a kitten but as loyal and as protective as a lion. Once they returned from their walk Ava and Bart would enjoy the latest gossip over tea. Ava always shared some baked goodies (no one could resist her apple crisp). Bart was amazed how Ava got around being blind and wheelchair bound. He figured she'd lived alone for so many years in her little home that she knew every nook and cranny.

Bart told Ava there were no updates to the mystery. She shook her head in disbelief. Then Mack walked right up to Bart and dropped a small shoe at his feet—they both froze. Bart asked Ava where Mack would have found a little shoe... "wait a minute!" they both said at the same time and with her permission he looked around inside the house then outside. Mack's dog house was full of shoes! The shoe mystery was solved— but how did Mack get a hold of everyone's shoes?

When he told Ava about all of the shoes in the dog house she laughed. They had figured that since Mack had his freedom at night he would find shoes at everyone's door. The neighbors were relieved to find out the culprit was innocent old Mack. From that day forward if their shoes went missing they knew where to look. Who knows Mack's reason for collecting stinky shoes but it turned out great for him because when someone came looking for their missing shoes they would take him for a nice long walk. ✳

Chapter 6

WHAT A PIG

I love animals of all kinds, but when it comes to owning one I tend to lean toward typical pets such as dogs and cats. Some creatures sure can be strange and in my experience I see this is especially true with cats. One minute they love you and purr on your lap and the next minute they jump off, stick their tiny nose up at you and prance away as if you never existed. Dogs on the other hand are much more loving and family oriented in general although there are always exceptions. We must have had at least a dozen cats and dogs over the years that ranged anywhere from a mangy critter roaming the streets, to those we inherited from relatives or friends that decided they didn't have time to care for their pets. I think we were a drop-off facility for both cats and dogs and other species but every little animal that came through our door lived happily until they went to animal heaven. My kids used to think that even fish and bugs went to heaven because they considered animals and all other species God's creatures and that we had been chosen to care for them. I never told them different.

I did try to draw the line when it came to caring for animals other than dogs or cats that I felt we couldn't manage such large farm animals.

My aunt had a little piggy, Mosley, and took care of him like a puppy until he grew into a huge pig. The animal control people threatened to take him away because of complaints from the neighbors. Mosley lived inside until he got too big and my uncle built him a pigpen. Neighbors complained about Mosley's odor and didn't like the sight of a pig rolling around in his own filth.

One day Mosley was outside and the neighborhood kids walked over to pet Mosley and give him an apple. Mosley was a gentle fella with stubby hairs on his back that felt like petting the bristles of a brush. But the kids loved the pig and took turns petting Mosley as he grunted with delight. All went well until the youngest child decided to join Mosley in the small rubber pool that was left for him to roll around in. It was certainly a sight to see a boy and a pig both squealing with joy and rolling around in that tiny pool which was barely big enough for Mosley. When the mother saw the muddy twosome she screeched in horror because not only was her kid covered head to toe in slop, but Mosley had just done his duty and filled the rubber boat with his "doo doo"! She immediately grabbed the poor kid out of the pool, grabbed a hose lying close, and sprayed the boy with cold water then dragged the screaming toddler home.

Even though the neighbors wanted him gone there was a reason for his leavin' that no one could argue; the sweet, adorable pig simply grew too big and could barely get through the door into the house and would run into the furniture and yes, he did poop inside. It's next to impossible to potty train a pig. Mosley ended up on a farm about 20 miles from his family and they could visit their darling pig whenever they wanted. In return for the farmers housing their beloved Mosley, Charles would drive out to the farm and help the folks when needed. It ended well for Mosley and his family and, no, they didn't make a ham out of Mosley. He died of natural casing...oops, *causes!* LOL :) ✻

Chapter 7

WHAT LURKS BELOW

Do you remember (as a kid) how scared you'd be of monsters hiding in the darkness under your bed? It wasn't just me, right? I remember getting a running start from the door and jumping into bed as fast as I could to not get my ankles grabbed. Being too afraid to check and risking being pulled under I would ask my brother if he would make sure the coast was clear. I insisted ... No! I *KNEW* that there was something under my bed. Yea, sure, he would make fun of me, but he'd always check it out before I went to bed.

As kids we'd believe just about anything anybody told us because (well, why not?) we were so innocent (and we trusted adults). The monsters that our young brains could conjure up were a sure thing back then and my brother knew what scared me. He loved to make me scream.

My parents would just laugh at me saying, "Your brother is teasing you." I wasn't too sure about that so I would offer him a quarter to check under my bed, inside my closet and behind the drapes. When the coast was clear he'd give me back my quarter but if not, he'd pretend to chase the thing out from under my bed and keep the quarter for his troubles. Best money I'd ever spent.

Some nights when he was too wrapped up in something or busy with his friends he'd tell me to go on to bed and to call him if I heard anything. Inside my room I would stand quietly in the doorway listening for any

PET TALES By Rachel Gies

sound, too afraid to check that dark abyss below my bed and when I was sure it was safe, quickly leap in and under the blankets in one fell swoop. For some reason, it seemed like the blankets made me a little safer and I'd eventually fall asleep. The next day my brother would ask "Didja see any monsters?" I'd tell him I did and I wanted my quarter back. Most kids go to bed and don't seem to be bothered by the thought of snakes or other creepy creatures underneath their bed, but for some it can be a very real and very scary experience.

One night I suddenly woke up with a start and heard this low growling underneath my bed. Luckily, my brother's room was next to mine and as frightened as I was I jumped as far as I could—airborne out of bed and ran to his room shaking. My grumpy brother wasn't thrilled about the wake up. Frantically whispering under my breath and in tears I got him moving. Reluctantly, he walked me back to my room muttering that it must have been a bad dream because he already chased away the wild things. How could he be so calm? We were all in danger! I wasn't about to breath another word as he bent down to look I stayed safe in the doorway, ready to run.

Now we both heard sounds from under my bed. When he turned on the light, got down on all fours and looked under the bed he saw two beady eyes staring back. For a moment I thought my brother was scared!

Then, from under the bed, the growl turned into a whine when Henry, our puppy saw my brother. He'd made it out of his box but was too little to jump on the bed so he crawled under it but got stuck behind a box of toys. He was probably just as scared as I was, not knowing exactly where he was. We both started laughing (me with relief but my brother was laughing at me!) Then he confessed that he locked the puppy in my room.

When I asked him why he just shrugged his shoulders and said he liked messing with my head.

Usually he was a pretty good guy who always watched out for me but believe me, eventually I got back at him and to this day he never knows what I have up my sleeve. It turns out the only creature I had to watch out for all those years was my prankster brother. ✳

Chapter 8

SMITTY THE KITTY

I remember when we got our first kitten. We named her Smitty, which was short for Smittendorf. We also referred to her as "little terror" and "feisty." Oh she was the most adorable kitten you ever saw. She was like a mini tigress, stripes and all with the cutest little paws and a pair of green, almond-shaped eyes that could stop you in your tracks. The lady who gave her to us was moving but needed to unload the latest litter. I guess Smitty's mom must have been pretty popular with the boy cats.

So we gladly brought Smitty home—ready to love and spoil her. We certainly did a great job of it too. She was so spoiled that she would spend her days sleeping and her nights running around the house like a maniac playing with her toys and tearing up anything she could get her sharp little claws into. If you fell asleep it wouldn't be for long because she'd pounce on your head or start hunting toes under the blanket with her tiny claws. I tried to keep her awake during the day, hoping she'd be too tired to run around all night. Not Smitty. She'd race from one room to another crashing into things. I could hear dishes rattle as she'd knock things off kitchen counters and dive into the sink smashing into pots and pans.

She was just a kitten and kittens usually outgrow their excessive drive to be active. And once we thought she was slowing down we put up our Christmas tree. She made that tree her jungle gym. I think every ornament I put on she knocked off and shattered. She'd race around it then kick up her

back paws and up the tree she flew like—Santa up the chimney. Had she sat in it quietly, she would have made a nice ornament. But instead she would rustle the branches until every piece of tinsel and ornament was shaken off. Twice, she managed to topple the tree down. We shouldn't have bought a fresh tree because with her shenanigans the needles fell off and covered the floor. By Christmas we had a naked tree of branches.

We had hoped that the first time the tree fell over she'd be too scared to climb it again. Like a climber to Mount Everest she was driven to get to the top at any cost. We even put a kiddie fence around the tree to keep her out of it. But, low and behold, there she'd be, staring at you from deep inside the tree. The following year we bought an artificial tree but, alas, things didn't change. She simply believed the tree was brought in for her.

The neighbor's dog, Boris, was a humongous Mastiff, as gentle as they come (as they say "he wouldn't hurt a fly") but always on a fairly lengthy leash. Smitty apparently knew this and took advantage of her good natured neighbor, she just loved to tease him. However, one particular afternoon someone either forgot to tie him up or he slipped out of his collar.

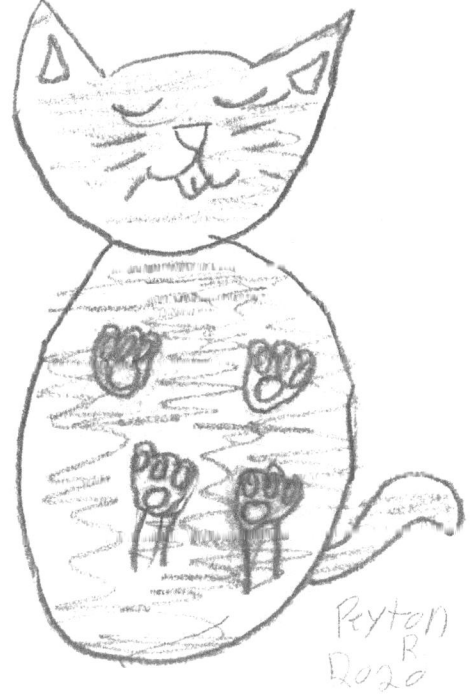

She snuck up on him as he slept peacefully on his own porch. Going for his snoozing snout she pawed at him with her furry little fists. Boris lifted his massive floppy-eared head and moaned at her for the rude awakening. This time he'd

PET TALES By Rachel Gies

had enough. He jumped up and went for the kill. Luckily, Smitty, small and agile, took off as if shot from a cannon. She screeched, Boris barked and both flew through the air. Things were moving so quickly It was like watching a cartoon in fast forward. Smitty zipped by us and disappeared high into the dark branches of a large pine tree. Thanks to the Christmas trees, she had trained well.

Boris's owner showed up to claim their poor, exhausted pooch. But Smitty wasn't coming down from that tree. Boris was bigger and faster than she thought and she'd never seen him move like that. We tried coaxing her down with a can of tuna and called to her sweetly, but nothing worked and it was starting to look like she'd never come down. Suddenly, as we were about to get a ladder, an innocent little squirrel appeared. Smitty spotted the squirrel and didn't think twice. I can still see that squirrel followed by that crazy cat tear across the busy road. We all covered our eyes as semi barely missed Smitty.

We weren't sure we'd see her again but by dinner time (*as if she knew*) Smitty came back looking a bit ragged and stressed out. Slowly she crept up the deck and gobbled up the can of tuna. She stretched out on the deck for a nap as if to regain her energy for the night shift.

It's said that cats have nine lives and that day we figured she'd gone through eight. She didn't dare tease Boris like she used to and she seemed to realize that she needed to be extra cautious with that ninth life. ✳

Chapter 9

MY BEST FRIENDS CHARLIE AND CHUCKIE

What was to be a quick shopping trip turned out to be an adoption of a life-long friendship. I was planning to go on vacation to visit with some of my relatives, which would be my first trip in some time. I had promised my family that I would come and celebrate the New Year with them. This required a trip to the mall, my favorite hangout, for several needed items.

I walked through a department store as I entered the mall and while making my way through swarms of people, I could hear dogs barking on the second level. *What would dogs be doing in a mall?* I thought. I was too busy to take the time to investigate and continued on my mission.

About an hour or so later I decided I had done enough damage for the day and was ready to head for home when I heard the barking again. It could be a guide dog, I thought, or maybe there was a pet show. Being an animal lover my curiosity got the best of me, so I walked towards where I heard the barking.

When I got to the shop I was surprised at what I saw. Inside one of the stores there were at least a dozen dogs. There were all kinds of beautiful dogs; some big and several little ones in a range of different breeds.

I asked someone standing close by what was going on and the person informed me that this was PAWS, one of Chicago's largest no-kill shelters. This organization finds good homes for these sweet orphaned dogs.

PET TALES By Rachel Gies

I had no intention of getting involved but there was one dog that caught my eye. He was a small black woolly looking cutie who watched my every move. I was still avoiding eye contact when I realized this dog reminded me of my beloved pet Charlie, a black poodle who had died several years ago. I loved him so much that I had sworn never to get another dog.

Oh, but I was wrong. This goofy little poodle, who was now jumping all around was kissing my hands trying to get me to look into his eyes.

I had to go home. I still had a lot of packing to do. I was planning to leave in three days. There was no way I could take this dog with me. Yet I could feel my heart starting to melt. Then the woman told me his name was Chuckie. Goocher! My Charlie had to be related they were absolutely identical! *What was I thinking?* I wasn't! I paid the fees for the puppy and thanked the people who had been caring so well for him but it seemed like a dream. On the ride home we glance at each other occasionally and I believe it became a real bonding experience for both of us. I realized I was becoming a mommy to a dog I just met and at the same time I was thinking about the trip I had planned and what I was going to tell my family.

Once home I was concerned about this little thing's well being. I picked up some dog food along the way and watched as he hungrily ate every morsel. I gave him some water and he drank what seemed to be enough to fill a bathtub. That night I called my family, who were very understanding. I still knew they thought, 'Here she goes again, trying everything possible to get out of coming for a visit'. I guess I was never much of a traveler.

I kept my eye on this poor thing because he looked so ragged after being at a shelter for months. I made him a soft bed in the kitchen. I didn't even know if he was potty trained. The following day we went to the local vet who gave Chuckie Too, as I called this little critter, a clean bill of health, and another bill for the exam. The doctor also informed me that this dog

was a miniature poodle and weighed just 11 pounds. I knew he needed care, good food and lots of love.

Next, I dropped him off at the groomer. When I returned a couple of hours later I couldn't believe how adorable this dog was. He was the mirror image of my original Charlie. I wondered if his personality would be anything like the first Charlie, who was a feisty critter. I remember how three of the veterinarians drew straws when Charlie came in for his shots. None of the vets liked that his bite could be worse than his bark.

However, Chuckie Too was a sweet dog and everyone fell in love with him. We became best buds. He loved going places with me and I even took him shopping with me. After all, we were still bonding.

Upon seeing Chuckie Too, people would ask where I got this cute little puppy. Always being the entertainer I'd say, "Oh, they are giving away puppies, today only, over by the stuffed toys. You buy two toys and get a free puppy." Of course several people would run back looking for the free puppies.

I finally managed to visit my family about three months later, but I missed my best friend. Chuckie is now happy and healthy and has gained eight pounds since. Just do me a favor, don't tell Chuckie he's a dog and not a person. ✱

Me & Charlie (or Chuckie)

Chapter 10

TRAINING HENRY

Pets are the companions we need because they love unconditionally, listen without talking back, they don't judge, and they require very little in return. Whether you have one or several kinds of pets, there is nothing like coming home and being greeted by a dog, cat, canary, gerbil or other furry friend and to share some one-on-one playtime, talking or even cuddling.

My friend Martha had a Westie named Henry. He is an adorable little guy with boundless energy and an appetite for mischief. A Westie (short for West Highland Terrier) has a sweet little face and looks innocent and so cuddly it's easy to forget they can be just as mischievous as any other dog. Of course he instantly became part of the family and loved by all, even on those days when it seemed he couldn't get into enough trouble. They had planned on him slowing down sooner, but those weren't Henry's plans. He loved life and he really loved chewing anything he could get a hold of.

Training Henry was so very hard Martha's hubby, Mel was ready to tear his hair over the cost of replacing things he destroyed. They confined Henry to a small hallway with "wee wee" pads for accidents because he had no intention of doing his civic doody outside. Here Henry had enough room to move around and it had tiled flooring instead of carpet. But even though he had plenty of chew toys and pee pads when confined Henry spent his time ripping off the wallpaper.

They moved him into the kitchen where there wasn't any wallpaper to tear up. For a few days things seemed to go pretty good. But when you can tear up wallpaper what's to stop you from shredding up a painted wall? From there they moved Henry into the den where it would be a little more comfortable for him, gated under a desk with the plastic floor protector. There was even a little doggy bed and the kids turned on the television to help keep him company when they left for school.

It was here that Henry's destruction turned to technology and he ate cords, chargers, the mouse to the laptop, anything he could reach. Martha thought it was her own fault because she should have known to put the stuff out of reach.

Two years passed and he was still wild and crazy chewing up stuff like a puppy. But once Henry did stop chewing on things he turned ornery and began to nip at others, including people. If someone came to the house that he did not know he tried to bite them and had to be crated. My friend wasn't sure what was worse, the chewing things and friends or wanting to tear apart every neighborhood dog that walked by.

Finally, the family thought long and hard about what they weren't doing right. Henry needed more attention. He needed a schedule, to be fed on time and always have water. He needed more walks. He needed to be around people as much as he was alone all day. They all agreed to devote more time and attention to Henry. By his third birthday he settled down.

Time heals all wounds and they were finally able to look back over the years, and laugh. The family really adored him. Training Henry has been quite an experience. They realized Henry was training them to keep their things picked up, take him out on time, and feed him before he ate what he shouldn't. Dogs really do try to communicate but if you're not used to seeing the signs, then you don't see the signs.

PET TALES By Rachel Gies

Hang in there if you have a puppy. Always remember the next time one trains you; it will keep getting better as long as you stay a step ahead. Enjoy the fun parts, laugh at the frustration, and relax in the love. Don't give up on a puppy. They don't come with directions and they don't know the rules! Seems it was Martha and Mel who took three years to train and not Henry! We just adore our pets don't we? ✱

Scarlet V.

Chapter 11

YODA AND GIUSEPPE

Yoda and Giuseppe were a real pair of trouble makers. They couldn't be in the same room for more than two minutes without getting into it. All they'd have to do was look at each other, and the fur would fly. Did I mention Yoda and Giuseppe were animals? Yoda was a clever little feline, no one knew what breed she was but she definitely had a mean streak. Giuseppe, was a sweet, rule following golden retriever. He would always wipe his paws before entering through the doggy door. But that was when (waiting patiently inside the door knowing the canine's routine) Yoda would attack. A simple plan of attack—always a surprise. Never knowing when or where Yoda would be hiding Giuseppe was always on guard. Giuseppe would poke his nose in first (an attempt to see if the coast was clear). As soon as his head came through the door Yoda would pounce on the poor unsuspecting beast punching at him with her paws of sharp nails.

At first the owners didn't know who to blame for all the fighting because the little kitty behaved angelically in front of them, but as soon as they turned their back Yoda acted on her hostility towards Giuseppe. Poor dog, he was so friendly and would never hurt a fly but for some strange reason Yoda took an immediate dislike towards him since they brought him home as a puppy. Everyone fussed over the little pup at first; oohing and aahing over the adorable blonde runt. Yoda was bigger than Giuseppe for the first few months and so she terrorized the little thing right from the start.

PET TALES By Rachel Gies

As Giuseppe grew into a beautiful big dog he was still intimidated by Yoda. Giuseppe never realized what his size meant and could have taken Yoda down without a problem. Sometimes Giuseppe would quietly nap after a long day of outdoor play, but once Yoda spotted the unsuspecting pooch she'd plot her revenge. She even went as far as eating his food. Another one of Yoda's favorite game was sitting quietly on the arm chair waiting and watching for the sweet canine to pass. Once Giuseppe walked past the chair she'd rock back and forth in anticipation and pounce on his back clinging tightly with her nails buried deep into the dog's fluffy coat. Poor Giuseppe would run around trying to shake the annoying creature off of him until someone would pull her off. It was a nightmare at times and no one knew what to do. They often had to be separated until everyone calmed down. Both animals were fiercely loved and the family hoped the two would learn to get along but the fiasco went on for too long.

One fateful morning everything changed. Yoda went outside for her stroll in the yard. Until that day she thought everyone understood that she was the queen of the animal kingdom. As she strutted around pouncing at the birds and chipmunks she didn't realize she was being watched. Hiding in the bushes a fox followed Yoda as she stretched out licking her paws and washing her whiskers. Out of nowhere the fox grabbed Yoda by the neck. Screeching bloody murder Yoda fought to free herself from the fox's jaws but to no avail. The more she struggled the tighter the jaws got.

Inside, Giuseppe made his way to the door for his morning doody. His ears perked up when he heard the commotion outside.

Without a thought for his own safety, Giuseppe sprang into action and ran straight for the fox, growling ferociously and barking up a storm. Frightened of the much bigger opponent the fox dropped the cat and scurried off. Shocked and stunned, Yoda crawled into the house bleeding and whining in pain. One of the kids caught the end of the attack as the fox disappeared over the fence. All hailed Giuseppe as a hero for saving Yoda's life.

Luckily, Yoda was okay other than some fur loss, a torn ear and bent tail. Animals have great instincts and Yoda knew Giuseppe had saved her. From that day forward the two actually became friends, even though they would fight now and then it was much more playful and friendly. They'd roll around on the floor in a mock fight with even more drama (no nails).

We don't always give our pets enough credit for understanding. Some animals have proven to show great intelligence. Perhaps we should pay closer attention. They could teach us all a few lessons in getting along. *

Anna Miller

By: Lila Huotari
Story: Sharing Laddie

Chapter 12

SHARING LADDIE

Dogs are often referred to as man's best friend but we know they are women's best friend too. One of my very favorite stories is the one about Laddie, a beautiful Collie with a long soft mane that would make one green with envy to have all that beautiful hair. Laddie was a wonderful companion for Harriet and Lester and their daughters Mary and Jane. Both girls grew up with their beloved pet and would argue as to who would get Laddie when they left home because they both loved the dog from the time he was just a 6-week-old puppy. They finally settled their argument by promising to share custody of Laddie which sounded crazy but it had to be worked out to keep peace in the family. Each girl would have Laddie every other weekend. You'd think they were sharing custody of a child but, silly as it seemed, that's how they worked it out so that they could each spend time with sweet Laddie.

Eventually both girls married but did not move far from their parents. When Jane got Laddie the first two weeks she spoiled him terribly by giving him too many treats. But when Mary had him the poor dog ended up in the hospital. Mary was a whiz at cooking Italian and baked a beautiful lasagna. As she took the lasagna out of the oven and set the pan on the counter to cool she got a phone call and walked out onto her front porch. After the call she got sidetracked again pulling a few weeds and cutting some flowers for the table. Back in the kitchen she found an empty lasagna

PET TALES By Rachel Gies

pan and a guilty looking Laddie. Evidently big enough to stand on his hind legs he had gobbled up the lasagna and licked the pan clean. Frantically, she took him to the vet who advised that the dog would be ok but she would have to endure some pretty stinky gas.

The arrangement with Laddie changed when Jane was expecting her first child and Mary kept Laddie with her until baby Michael was born. Unfortunately, baby Michael turned out to be allergic to long haired pets and so Laddie stayed with Mary.

Jane wanted to see Laddie if only for a few minutes now and then, but even that proved to be too tough on baby Michael. When Laddie got near Michael his little eyes would swell up and turn red. Mary was happy enjoying Laddie but started feeling a bit guilty about not sharing the dog with Jane anymore.

Laddie found a girlfriend named Muffy who belonged to one of the neighbors. No one was sure exactly what kind of dog Muffy was but she happened to have very short hair and didn't shed.

After a few months passed Muffy gave birth to four adorable puppies. When the neighbor asked Mary if she would like one of Laddie's pups she said "YES!". These cute little critters turned out to have very short hair like their momma. Mary brought one of the pups to Jane hoping that maybe this one wouldn't cause an allergic reaction for Michael. Jane reluctantly took the pup who she named Oscar. Over time baby Michael showed no allergic reaction which was great news for the family.

When the sisters get together they always bring Laddie and Oscar. Laddie loves his Oscar and cleans the little guy and cuddles up to him during visitations. Much has changed over the years and today, Laddie is a great grandpa and has visits with at least three of his offspring on a weekly basis. Laddie was loved as much as he loved both human and beast. ✻

Chapter 13

BOOGIE AND BART

It was a frightening event hunting for Boogie and Bart. Who are Boogie and Bart you might ask? They are gerbil friends who shared a fairly roomy two story habitrail. The twosome received lots of love and care and even got the run of the house occasionally. Sammy and Casey, six-year-old twin brothers got them as a birthday surprise from their Grandpa because they were not allowed to have a dog in their condo. Mom and dad weren't too excited about the critters at first. Mom knew she would end up cleaning and feeding them.

Grandpa wouldn't listen to her complain and laughed with merriment, "Remember how many animals you had on the farm?" Sandy told her father that living on a farm is a lot different than living in a condo. And her father dismissed the comment and said "gerbils are a lot different than horses". They all couldn't help but smile as the twins squealed with joy at the sight of their gift.

Each day the kids would take turns feeding the gerbils. Mom coached the boys never to leave the door of the cage open. Then one day it happened. No one knows who left the door open but Bart and Boogie capitalized on the chance and escaped their confines. The boys came back with food and water for their pets and saw the open door. Neither boy wanted to admit or tell mom but they knew they had better find the creatures and get them back in their cage before their parents found out.

PET TALES By Rachel Gies

They searched everywhere in the corners of their room, their closet and between their toys both inside and out of the toy box. They found no trace of the gerbils. Now the boys decided they had better fess up. Sammy was more courageous of the two and told their Mom what happened, kind of ... He didn't want them to get into trouble so he tweaked the story just a bit.

Sammy told their mom that the neighbor's cat had gotten into the condo while they were getting water, opened the door of the cage and when they returned the cat ran out and the gerbils were gone.

Sandy sat the boys down and encouraged them to be truthful because Boogie and Bart needed to be found for their own safety. Just as the boys were about to fess up, a blood curdling scream came from the condo directly below them. *Uh, oh!* The three rushed down to Mrs. McCloud's condo.

Their mom knocked on the door that was opened by a shaky Mrs. McCloud. Sandy told the elderly woman that she didn't see mice in her home but the boy's gerbils who got away from them. Looking slightly relieved, she immediately allowed the three in to hopefully end their search. The boys called for Boogie and Bart as they walk/ran through the place.

Low and behold, there inside a basket of yarn, sat Boogie and Bart, huddled together, with their wiggling little button noses. Quickly, the boys snatched them up and holding them close ran back home to return them to theirs. Mom scolded them even though they learned their lesson. Having grown up on a farm she understood the love between a child and their pet. Sammy and Casey vowed that it would never happen again as they held their little hands over their hearts. If only she could get Boogie and Bart to make the same promise. ✱

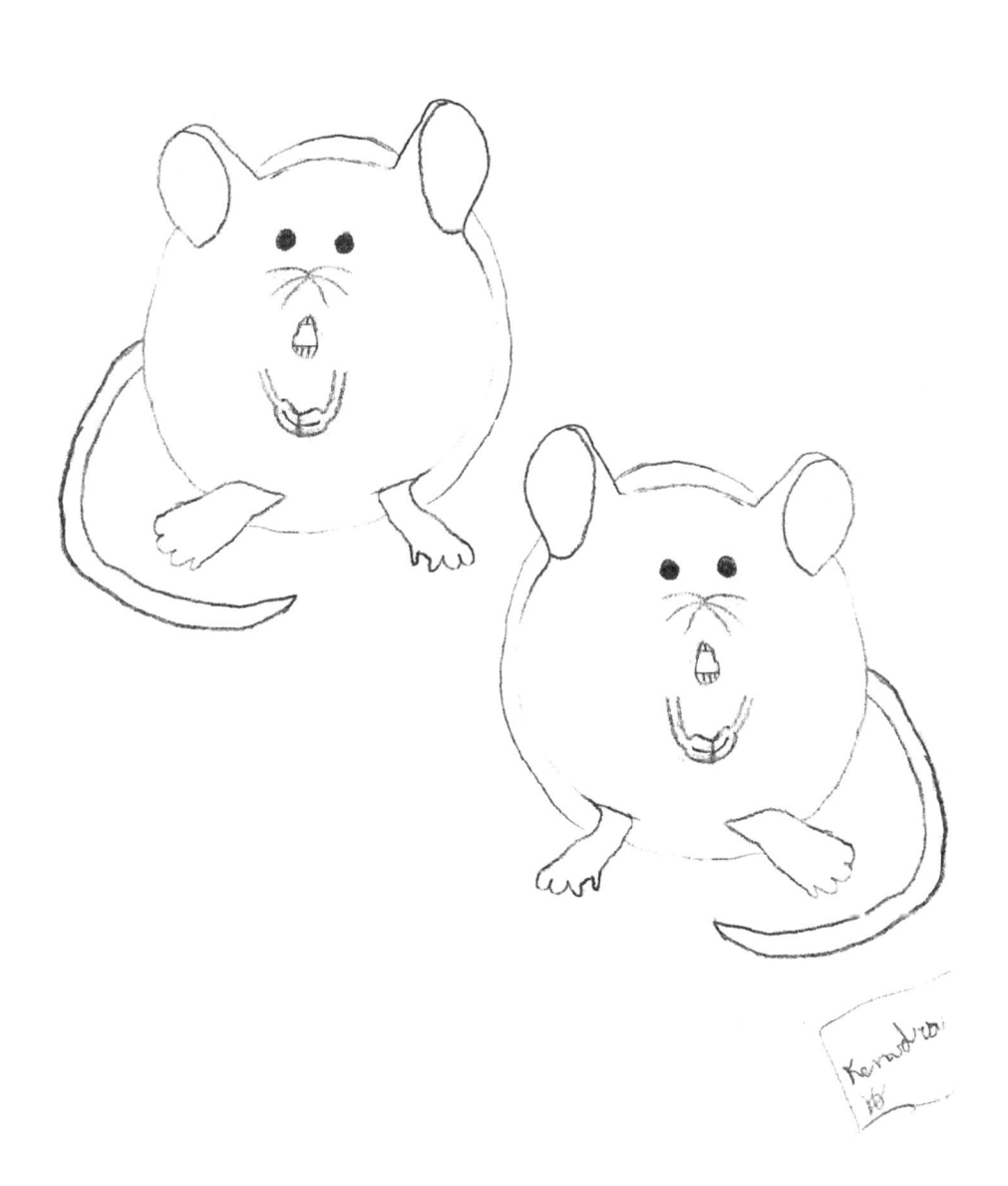

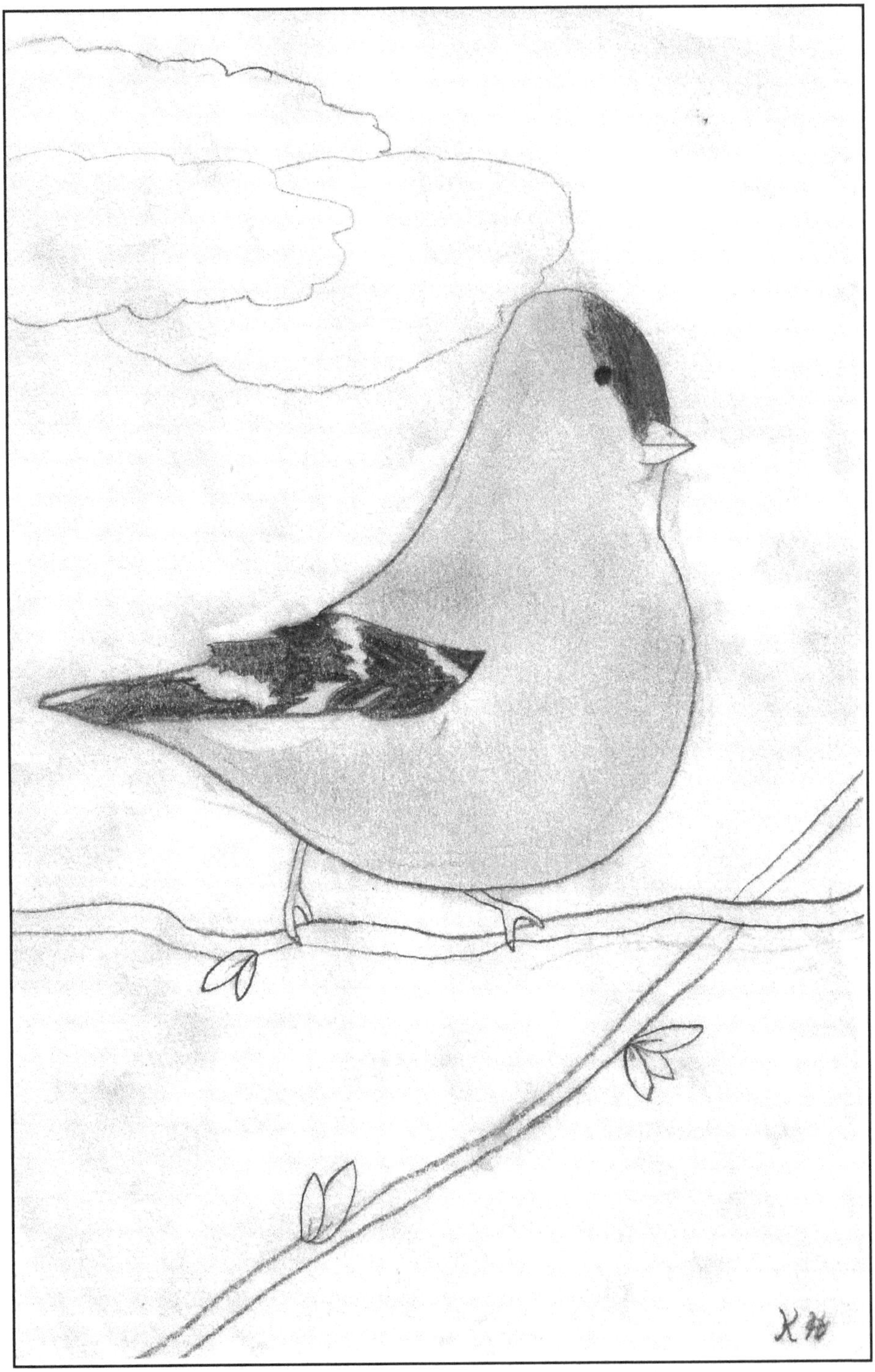

Chapter 14

GLASS KISSES

Once summer has come to an end and we prepare ourselves for a nasty cold winter there are some little things we will miss. For years we've had bird feeders in our yard welcoming birds of all kinds. There are small birdhouses where mamma's babies hatch in the spring. Nearby, papa birds frantically watch for danger, alerting his family of every threat and momma birds can be found in the yard searching for food for her feathered family.

Over the years, we've had many beautiful birds such as bluebirds, finches, cardinals, and robins chirping around the yard and tiny hummingbirds sipping on nectar. This has been such a delight for us watching these beautiful creatures at work filling up on food and returning the next day for more. It is also fascinating to watch them gather materials to create nests because they use just about anything they can find. They are incredible members of the circle of life sharing their beauty and grace. This assortment of birds that partake in their timely gathering and departure is like watching a rhythmic dance. Some become a little aggressive but for the most part they seem to get along and have a special hierarchy known only to them.

One little bird in particular has been such a delight to watch this year. The family would gather at the window for the feathered entertainer to put on a show. A bright yellow and black goldfinch who returned to eat at our kitchen window feeder then perch on the thermometer shaped like a

PET TALES By Rachel Gies

cat. He'd return several times a day and seemed to stare right at you then peck at the glass over and over. Perhaps, the goldfinch has come to know me since I spend so much time at the kitchen window watching him. He seemed fearless and something very special occurred one day. As we stared at each other through the glass I moved my finger along the window toward the goldfinch and gently tapped back at him. His tiny beak and my fingers would meet as he tapped back as if giving kisses. I so enjoyed our little game I started calling this "the glass kiss."

This little bird brought me peace and many smiles to my sometimes crazy-busy life and I looked forward to seeing him. I have always found birds to be beautiful creatures but this little guy gave me a deeper appreciation of them. The little details in their colors, movements and sounds are incredible and so very unique. I hate the thought of them leaving for another season and can't wait for their return.

Since writing this story of my new found friend, the goldfinch has stopped coming to my window. I suppose he has gone south for the winter and is bringing someone else a special glass kiss. His little glass kisses were such a wonderful, moving experience I hope that somewhere, someone else is relishing in the beauty of it.

Once I shared my story I found out that my grandkids and a neighbor also have received glass kisses. I used to worry about the birds in the winter but know I look forward to the glass kisses that spring will bring. ✻

Chapter 15

VET TO GO

Going to the veterinarian is nothing new to a pet owner because just like everyone they need medical attention or regular checkups to stay healthy. We love our pets and are willing to spend as much as we have to and hopefully we can afford whatever it takes.

Whenever we adopted a pet we instantly knew we'd have to find a reliable vet. I know we've spent more on vet bills than on a year's worth of groceries. My old Uncle Herman claims he spent more on his three dogs than he did replacing his teeth. Our family has brought home anything that walked, crawled and slithered. There was so much love for our animals because they were an integral part of the family. Dogs, cats, gerbils, mice, and rats, just to name a few. We even housed a pair of giant turtles at one time when one of the kid's teachers needed a place for them. Of course my kids volunteered immediately. So, for the next three months, we had turtles in a box. I kept our tomcat Miles well fed in the hopes he wouldn't snack on Molly and Arminus. We had to keep the turtles downstairs and keep the basement door closed at all times.

In the meantime our stray cat Muzo was in a cat fight one night and needed emergency surgery on his ripped ear, torn up tail, bleeding nose and scratched eye ball. After being patched up the poor thing resembled Quasimodo and scared the day lights out of everyone. He looked so bad, even the other cats stayed out of his way. We still loved him until he died at the age of 17. We held funerals for all of our critters when they passed on to

PET TALES By Rachel Gies

pet heaven. We had a backyard burial ground of shoe boxes.

When we saved Sam, our Pomeranian, he needed heart surgery and over half of his teeth removed due to a poor diet. By the time we were done, the money we spent on his vet bill would have paid for a boat.

Next, was Saul, the frustrated cockatoo who slept all day and yelped all night screaming obscenities at anyone who came through the door! He would imitate people when they talked repeating word for word but in a sarcastic mocking way.

Once Saul's cage was left open and Muzo came into the room. Saul landed on the back of the couch where Muzo usually took his nap. At first, Muzo didn't see the bird and crawled on the couch to take his usual snooze. Suddenly, Muzo must have heard something and opened one eye. Saul had accidentally, or maybe purposely dropped a bit of white wash into Muzo's eye and started chatting sassily. Muzo jumped up, caught Saul mid-take-off and prepared himself for supper. Saul fought and screeched bloody murder. With all of the commotion we ran into the room and almost witnessed the "killing of a mocking bird."

Luckily, we saved Saul in the nick-of-time but required another trip to the emergency vet. Poor Saul was pretty beat up and barely clung to life for three days. That vet bill was plenty high too and could have paid for a ticket to Paris.

We also had a gerbil named Emma who had some tough moments and needed medical attention. We couldn't figure out why she was so depressed just sitting there and barely eating, until we were told Emma was an Elmer and needed company. Then came Ali, a chubby gerbil the kids had traded for a hamster. It wasn't too long before there were baby gerbils crawling around.

So, even though the medical bills can be sky high, we keep bringing pets home and falling in love with them. For me it is worth every penny because they bring so much happiness and memories that last forever. I have rushed many of them to emergency clinics in the middle of the night but have never regretted it. Just like kids, we know the pocket book will be hit. I know if I added up our vet bills over the years the house would have been paid for a long time ago. However, what is a house without a wet nose to greet you, a deep purr to warm your heart, or a bird to mock you? It just isn't a home. ✽

Chapter 16

A HOME FOR MAC

Oscar lost his wife of 60 plus years following a long illness. Living only with his dog Mac, Oscar's children became concerned for his well being. He was a man in his 80s whose knee, leg and foot problems were only getting worse so their fears were well founded. Oscar used to work vigorously on a treadmill, used weights and swam at the local health club. This activity had to be scaled down considerably because of health problems. At the same time his hearing and eye sight was getting worse. His eye doctor suggested he stop driving. Oscar didn't like hearing this but realized his limitations.

He sold his car and agreed with his children that he should sell the house he and his wife had lived in for 30 years. Oscar needed to find a retirement home that would allow him to keep his 17-year-old dog, Mac. His family wanted the best for him and did not rush him into making this life changing decision. Oscar was a very independent man. He also knew that his children loved him very much. They found a place for him where he'd have activities and make friends.

At the same time the new apartment was being prepared for Oscar and Mac, his home was being emptied. His belongings were being donated which added to his unhappiness. Within the year since his wife passed away, he was losing his health, his mobility and now his home. However, he was keeping his best friend Mac and a few possessions he couldn't live without.

PET TALES By Rachel Gies

Mac was now the major concern because taking the dog outside a couple times a day could be a challenge with his limited mobility. Mac had trouble getting trained to do his business on papers in the bathroom, and Oscar had to get down on his hands and knees to clean it up. Then there was an incident where outside on a walk with Mac, Oscar tripped and fell. Mac stayed with his master until help arrived. Neighbors helped Oscar up and luckily he only had minor scrapes.

Oscar made many friends especially one of the employees, Inga, who had three dogs and a cat of her own. She saw the difficulty Oscar was having and offered to take Mac home with her to give Oscar a break. Mac was immediately accepted by Inga's dogs and cat. It was good timing because Oscar got the flu and ended up at the hospital.

Back home after a five day stay in the hospital Inga assured him that Mac was doing just fine and getting along with her pets. Inga said she would bring Mac back to Oscar but the dog was welcome to stay at her home as long as needed. Oscar admitted that Mack would be more comfortable with her but he did have trouble letting go of his faithful friend. Inga realized how difficult this must be for Oscar and invited him to her house so he could see how well Mac was doing in his new environment.

Oscar and his friend Bill drove out to Inga's. A den had been converted into a dog room where each dog had their own crate where the dogs were crated at night but otherwise had the run of the house. There was a sliding door to the deck and backyard where the dogs could do their business and play and sleep in the sun during the day. Inga, being a long time pet owner fed the dogs well.

Oscar could see that Mac was being well cared for. He was so well adjusted at Inga's home. Mac was so happy to see him and jumped into his lap slobbering all over him. Inga assured Oscar that if he wanted Mac back she would bring him anytime. But he refused the offer and felt this was a very good arrangement.

Oscar was very pleased that Mac was being well taken care of and they would be able to visit. Oscar felt that he finally found some comfort and peace again. Losing his life-long mate was terribly painful and when he thought he could no longer care for Mac it was even more devastating. Now he could relax knowing that Mac was in loving hands. Oscar slowly resumed his hobby of painting. He painted a portrait of old Mac so the first thing he would see every morning was his dearest friend. ✽

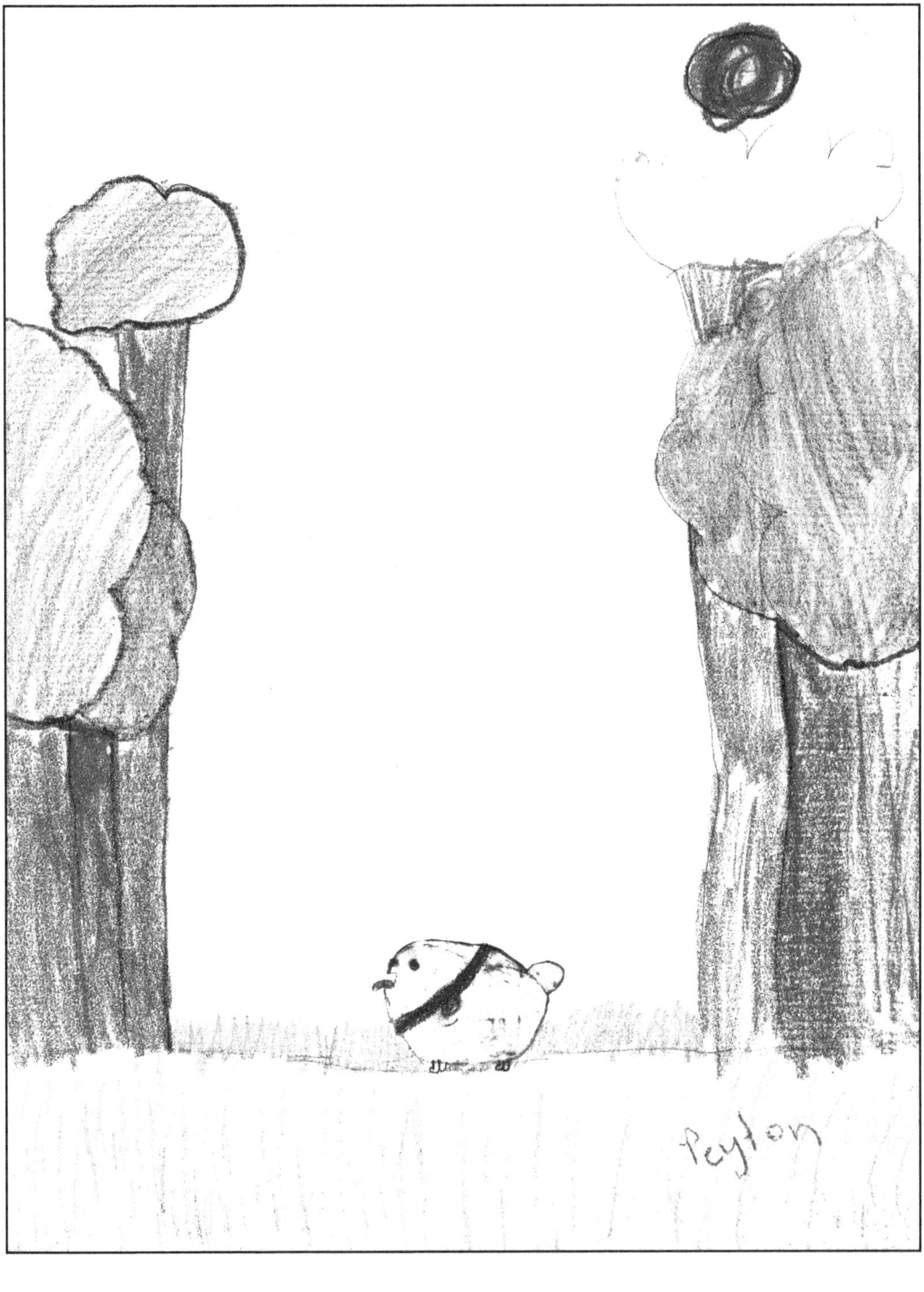
Peyton

Chapter 17

SPARKY

Sparky joined our family as a tiny pup. We immediately fell in love with him. Why did we name our puppy Sparky? Because his personality just sparkled! Sparky was about eight weeks old when we got to take him home and from day one everyone, including the other pets, accepted him as one of the family. At that time we had three cats, four dogs, six guinea pigs, and several multi-colored tropical fish. We loved them all.

Sparky was too small to roam around the house alone because we'd all trip over him and he'd get lost easy. When he couldn't find his way around he'd howl like a banshee. We would all rush to his rescue, pushing to be the first to save Sparky, be the little guy's hero, get the thank you face licks and excited body shakes. Occasionally, I would get up in the middle of the night and bring Sparky back to bed with me so that I'd have someone to cuddle when my hubby was out of town. I guess Sparky just gave all of us comfort, so sweet and fluffy. When he'd bury his tiny wet nose into our necks we felt so loved.

Sparky didn't grow much and to this day we still aren't sure what kind of dog he was. We found him at an animal shelter and they could only guess what kind of breeds were all mixed up in that adorable little body. All we really knew for sure was how much we loved the little fluffy ball of fur that felt soft like silk and a face that could make our hearts melt.

PET TALES By Rachel Gies

Everyone was supposed to take turns feeding and walking the pets, but as much as the kids loved them they were lazy and would fight over whose turn it was. When the kids fought, Sparky would retreat into the corner of the couch and bury himself in the cushions. We loved him too much to see him scared like that and so the arguing ended.

One warm summer evening as the sun was retreating into the horizon, Sparky, Leo the poodle, and Lester the terrier were enjoying the freshly cut grass while the kids played tag and I enjoyed the breeze and a book. Out of nowhere came a bunch of wild coyotes that sprang onto the lawn ready to snatch our dogs. They came as a pack which spelled danger. The smallest coyote was ready to pounce on Sparky who looked like a snack (he was so tiny). We all stood there paralyzed as Sparky, who had absolutely no fear of man nor beast, made eye contact with him. We knew he wouldn't stand a chance against any of them, let alone a whole pack.

Trying to keep calm I slowly moved to pick up Sparky and grabbed him mid-spring, just as he let out the biggest BARK his little body could make. At that very same moment my daughter let out a blood curdling scream that scared us all including the coyotes. My son grabbed the hose and turned it on the coyotes and they disappeared as fast as they had appeared. The whole scene took seconds but felt like time had stopped.

After that Sparky pranced around like he *knew*, his bark had saved his family. But to this day my daughter says it was her scream that saved us and my son still insists it was his precision hose-work.

Sparky, lived to the ripe old age of 19. Yes, you read it right. Sparky was the longest living pet out of five cats, seven guinea pigs and eight dogs throughout the years. I like to believe that all of our beloved pets are together somewhere having fun. Who knows, maybe Sparky has found some playful, *friendly*, coyotes. ✶

Chapter 18

WHEN WE LOSE A BELOVED PET

WARNING! SAD ALERT: This is a very sad story and I hope you don't have to go through this with a beloved pet but it may help to know you are not alone. I am sharing this because animal lovers know that to your pet, you are everything and dogs especially are all about you. Cherish that intense, unconditional love every minute you've got.

While not everyone owns a pet, the majority of us love having them and consider them an equal member of our family. Our furry, feathery, and scaly friends do so much for us just by being there and loving us unconditionally. We celebrate their birthdays and even buy them gifts. Being with them brings us joy and comfort but when we have to be apart it can break our hearts and thats the price we pay that is not monetary but emotional.

What is not right is that our pet's life span is so much shorter than ours. Perhaps there is a reason in this, for us to fall in love with more than one pet in our lifetime. That means at the end of their life we may have to make a decision, a very sad decision. When the quality of life is no longer what you wish it to be for your friend and you'd rather not have the option to decide when they have had enough and see them go in peace.

For instance when my Smitty was no longer in control of herself and couldn't even get up on her own. She was miserable and I hoped she was not in pain. She looked like a helpless kitten again and I found it hard to make

PET TALES By Rachel Gies

eye contact but when I did her life flashed before my eyes. She had been a cherished family member and by my side forever it seemed.

As nature dictates, she just got old, she couldn't keep her food down and could barely stand up much less make it to her litter box. After all she was 18 years old which is a long life for most domestic animals. Looking at her, she was still a beautiful mix of exotic colors, those big eyes lined in black that squinted happily at a simple pet of her head. She grew up with my children and grandchildren and was adored by all. I knew she couldn't go on like that. She'd still look at me with those big, loving, trusting eyes.

I took her to the vet's office hoping they would find some miracle cure for old age and after waiting for tests and a few prescriptions life was good ... at least for a little while. The vet said that she had some time left and to watch for certain signs. "Keep her comfortable". A cloud of dread hung over my head. Time was running out. I still dared to hope and every morning I'd run to see if she was better and halfway there my heart would stop and my feet would slow at the thought of the alternative.

Well intending friends share opinions

By: Lila Hubbard

that don't help or make me feel any better. I know inside my heart that no matter who I talk to it's my decision and mine alone. They can't tell me anything I don't already know.

I agonized about when to do it. Tomorrow? Next week? I'm told as long as the animal still eats there's time, but I've seen her quality of life diminished. Her food intake is barely a teaspoonful. Is it time to let go? Do I make an appointment or just take her to the vet now? The vet says I'll know when the time comes. He offers to check Smitty for kidney failure so he can put her on a dialysis machine. How scary and stressful for this slight, tired creature to end her days on a machine. Is it worth it? How could he offer this option that clearly isn't an option? Now I have to say "no" to this? Would this machine bring her back at 18 years old? Of course not and deep down I know (and so does the vet). The reality is that she is suffering and I am too. While I think I know what is best for her I'm willing to hold on just to have her a little while longer and not be the one to end her days. I prayed for divine intervention.

Then that dreaded day arrived. Carefully I carried our precious little Smitty who had been a family member through four Presidents, kids and grand kids and brought joy to all of our lives. She was wrapped lovingly in her pink fluffy blanket that she always loved. I stood outside the door with a heavy heart and slowly walked inside the building knowing that she won't be leaving with me. Oh man! I'm really trying not to cry. People are watching as I enter. The sympathetic office girl leads me to a room and I wait. Alone the tears can't be stopped. What is taking so long? Part of me wanted to get up and leave with her. I wondered if this waiting period was planned so that I could have a little more time with her or just enough time to change my mind and run. This is by far one of the worst things I've ever had to do.

PET TALES By Rachel Gies

Time passed and even though I was told the doctor would be with me shortly, it is an eternity. I was trying to get the tears out before someone came in. She must have been in pain because she meows every time I shift her in my arms. Softly, I whisper to her that soon she'll be out of pain. She looks up at me and it seems as if she senses that this is goodbye. I apologize and thank her for choosing me. I could almost hear the beat of her weak heart but its my own that's beating so hard.

Suddenly, the door of the small room opened and a somber looking vet walks inside. He already knows that few words are needed and I'm grateful for this. He understands my pain and respects it. Mindlessly I pet her as the vet explains what's going to happen. She won't feel anything. I nod as the vet injects her with the sedative. I look away because the last thing I want is for her to feel any more pain. Then I look down at my beloved Smitty as the light goes out in her cloudy but once beautiful eyes. The next shot is the last shot. She is gone and no more. No words are needed. I turn to leave barely realizing I'm crying because there is numbness with the pain. Tears are streaming down my face and I don't care who sees them. At last, no more pain. She is in her well deserved resting place. Painful as it was for me I have to believe I made the best choice for her because

I loved her dearly. I gave her the best life I could. At least we had each other to comfort, in life and death. ✱

Chapter 19

GOIN' ON A GUILT TRIP

Animals are so in tune with each other and their environment. For example, when you're planning on leaving them for a few days it is as if they can read your mind. Take old Chuckie, my sweet little pooch who knows whenever I'm planning a little trip, especially when it's for more than one day. While he is not a mind reader it does make me wonder if animals have a sixth sense and just instinctively know when something is up or going to occur.

Usually, I run in and out of the house all day long, and Chuckie just sleeps his time away, paying little attention to my comings and goings. But when I plan a trip somehow he knows!!! How he knows is a mystery to me. They are known to have an uncanny ability when there's a storm brewing or if someone is approaching before anyone else hears anything.

I was planning to leave for a few days and could swear that Chuckie knew. I tried acting nonchalant around him as if I wasn't even thinking about my trip. However, there it was, the crazy sixth sense that kicked in, and I could tell because he followed me every step I took. He'd stare at me as if to say, "I know you're leaving me ..." I ignored him and yet I felt a sense of guilt knowing he'd have to stay somewhere else. It's weird that he even knows when he has to see the vet because he starts a little hiding routine and acts like a nervous wreck. His fur seems to just fly off of him from all the stress.

PET TALES By Rachel Gies

With dread, I knew the time had come for me to pack. I dragged up the old suitcase for my trip to Europe, but before I even opened the door from the basement, luggage in hand, Chuckie was already displaying quite an attitude. He sat there staring at me as if I had forgotten to feed him. That sad look in his eyes almost made me change my mind about going, but I needed to go, and as bad as I felt about it he couldn't come with me.

I dragged my suitcase up the stairs and he followed right behind me, literally on my heels. He's lucky I didn't knock him back down the stairs. I opened the suitcase on the floor and began filling it up. When I turned around Chuckie was looking up at me inside my suitcase with a look as if to say, "Whadaya you gonna do about it?" His dark beady eyes glared at me, never leaving me as he scrutinized my every move! *Okay*, I thought, *time to get him out of there*. I lifted his small furry body and placed him on the floor. Not a chance! He hopped right back inside.

I put the suitcase on the bed and continued packing. Chuckie, being an elderly dog, even though he behaved like a naughty pup, couldn't jump up on the bed anymore. Even though that little problem was solved, he continued to follow my every movement to the point that I started feeling even more guilty about leaving him behind. Thinking of bringing him along would still be out of the question at his age. He was not a healthy dog and had been plagued with diabetes for the last 5 years. Glaucoma had developed in one eye and a cataract in the other. He also suffers from a disease of his liver and requires much tender loving care and lots of medication. Not exactly a good candidate for traveling overseas.

I had made an appointment with the veterinarian where he would stay for the duration of my trip. As much as I hated leaving my little sweet guy, I did have to take this trip and that was final. I tried convincing myself that leaving him behind was good for him and that he would get the best of care at the vet. When I finally finished packing, Chuckie had a look of defeat on his cute, little face and seemed to be saying with his big black eyes: "Ok, you go girl."

He was a welcomed guest at the vet where most of the young assistants had taken a liking to Chuckie. I might even say that he was their favorite guest but they probably make everyone feel that way. As soon as Chuckie and I walked inside the clinic, the girls fawned over him as if he had entered a beauty contest and won first place. They "OOHed and AAHed" over him during which time the tongue popped out of his mouth and I could have sworn he was smiling back at them. I think if he could talk he might say to me, "See ya later!" He immediately lost interest in me and my trip and when I was returning seemed no longer any concern to Chuckie. *He could have at least acted as if he'd miss me, couldn't he?*

My trip was fun but I missed my little guy. I called the vet check in on him. I bombarded the poor girl with questions: *"How's Chuckie doing? Is he eating? Is he okay? Does he act happy?"* I was dying to hear the answers but couldn't stop asking questions.

She answered my questions and even offered to go back and check on him to let me know how he was doing at the moment. I told her it wasn't necessary. I just wanted to know how he was doing (*without me*, I thought to myself). I should have known that he'd be in good hands ... *the girls absolutely adored him.*

The first thing I did when I got home was pick him up. I was excited and couldn't wait to see him. I figured he'd missed me terribly. First I took care of his bill and the girls brought out his bag with his meds, his food, treats, bowls and his toys. The only thing missing now was Chuckie. Tears welled up as I saw my sweet, lovable, lonely Chuckie emerge from the back room. *We were apart for a whole week!* He must have been so lonely and

PET TALES By Rachel Gies

depressed wondering why I left him. Will he forgive me?

But I couldn't have been more wrong—Chuckie trotted right past me. Talk about your cold shoulder. I'd seen more excitement from him after I'd returned from a quick errand. Was I disappointed? Of course I was! Guess I missed him more than he missed me. My instinctive little dog taught me something that day that I should have known all along; It's all about him. ✻

Chapter 20

CAT BATH

As with all kids one never knows what they might be getting into when no one is watching. Or maybe when all seems too quiet there may be a little trouble brewing? This episode could have been a scene from *Home Alone*.

My friend, Joe was watching his 4-year-old son Dino, while his wife had gone off to do some shopping. Now we all know how things go when daddy watches the kids. It isn't that they don't pay attention, but sometimes daddy may be occupied or engrossed in that long awaited ball game.

The family lived in a large beautiful two story home with lovely furnishings all throughout. The floors were made of solid oak and exotic rugs beautifully covered them. They had several pets because Dino's family wanted him to grow up with animals. Dino loved his dog, Robo, and his new little kitty, Tipper, two parakeets, Leo and Nellie, and a hamster named Jake. Robo was a Chesapeake Bay retriever, and liked to nap in the early evenings because he ran outside all day chasing rabbits around the yard and squirrels up trees. Dino loved his pets and didn't feel like an only child because they were members of the family. Dino and Robo were best pals and enjoyed playing outside.

Tipper was the newest addition of the family and played mostly by herself catching flies and swatting at Robo's long floppy tail. She was a free spirit and already showed everyone who's boss. Dino would pick Tipper up and carry her all over the house until she got fed up and showed those

PET TALES By Rachel Gies

small but sharp kitten claws. She'd escape and hide outside for hours trying to avoid being captured again. Dino finally gave up the chase and started playing with his little match box cars, and his Thomas trains until he tired and looked for something else to do. As an only child, he was a happy little boy and usually found ways to entertain himself. He had lots of toys, but you know when kids get bored they get tired of playing with the same things and start exploring other avenues.

Tonight Dino decided he'd look for something else to stimulate his little mind and do something that was more fun than the same old toys and games. He wanted to play with daddy but he was busy watching TV. He could have sat with his dad to watch the game but being just 4 years old the game wouldn't hold his interest for long. Dad told Dino during the break they would have ice cream assuming that would suffice so he could focus on the big game. That was all Dino needed to hear and off he went on an adventure. Dino climbed upstairs while daddy's attention continued to be riveted on the game. He went into the bathroom where he spotted Tipper nestled comfortably in the corner of the shower stall.

Since they had brought the kitty home she always liked to snooze inside the shower stall. No one knew why she liked crawling in there, but she obviously found comfort there or perhaps she felt she was in a safe haven away from Dino's grabby little hands. Dino wanted to play with her and decided that maybe Tipper could use a bath. After all, to a 4-year-old, what other reason could there be for the kitten to curl up in the shower. Dino was a very gentle child and would never hurt his animals but given his age, he did things the way it made sense to him, not realizing the consequences of his actions.

Dino climbed inside the shower stall where Tipper lay curled up in a tiny fur ball. Several shampoo bottles were sitting in the shower caddy and

Dino had easy access to all products. He closed the glass shower doors and reached for a bottle. Tipper froze and waited for her opponent's next move because she knew something was up. His little hands worked the cap off and squirted shampoo up and down the cat. Tipper jumped up shaking off the offensive goop. Dino opened the other bottle and poured more shampoo over the kitty and then rubbed it in until clouds of suds appeared everywhere. It was hard to tell there was a kitten underneath all those soap bubbles.

    Dino was having a blast. Tipper however, was not. The cat searched desperately, looking for an escape. Dino tried to hold her but had a tough time with the slick feline. He squealed with delight and started lathering himself up too. Next, he turned on the water faucet. Dino was splashing and jumping among all the suds as the water rose to the top of the tub. Tipper had reached her absolute limit. Her tiny front paws batted at the shower door in a frantic effort to get out. Finally, Dino opened the door slightly, and Tipper managed to squirt out from the shower. Child and beast both took off running throughout the house with clouds of fluffy suds flying every which way.

    The kitty flew downstairs taking cover as Dino howled for the kitty to stop. He had grabbed his mom's blow dryer to dry off Tipper's coat. Soap suds were everywhere and Dino was now crying. Dad finally heard the commotion and came out to see what was going on. He took one look at the scene before him and quickly realized what had happened. Now all three of them were running around the house sliding on the slippery floors.

    When at last Joe caught up with Dino he asked, "Whoa, what is going on?" There stood Dino, dripping wet trying to tell his side of the story. His little lower lip was quivering as he tried to explain that Tipper was sleeping inside the shower cause she wanted a bath. Dino looked up at his dad with

PET TALES By Rachel Gies

large blue eyes and a big grin on his half toothless mouth. His turned up face was priceless. Joe couldn't help but laugh at the sight before him. Here was his kid dripping with soap from head to toe. Luckily, Joe got a hold off the soapy, dripping kitten and managed to hang onto her. Once Joe rinsed and dried the poor creature it ran under the couch where she was sure to be safe from Dino. Meanwhile, something was starting to run down the carpeted steps and Joe realized immediately something else was happening upstairs. He took the wet stairs two at a time and came to a screeching halt when he saw water pouring out of the tub. *Oh no!* He splashed across the watery soaked floors into the bathroom and quickly shut off the water. "Wait until your mother gets home," Joe said in an exasperated voice. But he knew that he was in just as much trouble since this happened on his watch.

When mom got home Dino and Joe had already mopped up most of the water damage. They both confessed. After mom found out what had happened she couldn't help but laugh at the comical situation. Yes, it seemed that both Dino and Daddy had learned a valuable lesson in her absence. They explained to Dino that kitties do not need baths. Dino protested "Robo gets a bath?" Joe and Megan explained that dogs do get baths but kittens bathe themselves. Dino said, "Can I give Robo a bath?" Joe and Megan laughed and promised Dino that the next time Robo needed a bath he would be the first to know and Mommy would need to be home to supervise. ✱

Chapter 21

STRAY CATS

Living out in the country Jesse and his wife Shelly enjoyed the company of a couple stray cats they named Max and Karl. They met these skinny little creatures when they bought their house in the country many years ago. Both strays wandered into the couple's yard one day. At first, Jesse thought they were rats because he had grown up in the city and they resembled rodents sneaking around. Jesse always had a soft spot for animals but couldn't keep pets because he was terribly allergic. Their home was a large cottage style farmhouse with a lot of room, but they had to stay outside. He saw to it that they were always well fed and had plenty of fresh water to drink. When Jesse worked outside his buddies would follow him around patiently.

These cats must have been living in the neighborhood and surviving on scraps that people threw out because they were fully grown. From day one, both felines made themselves known to Jesse and Shelly and visited every night. It's as if they knew that the new owners of the house would take care of them. As skinny as they were the little critters seemed so vulnerable. Whenever Jesse came home from work he was greeted by Max and Karl. They seemed joined at the hip. When one cat came out of the woodwork, the other one would follow right behind.

The names were given by Shelly, who also immediately fell in love with them. The cats seemed very intelligent, street smart. Max and Karl knew when it was chow time and they'd come running licking their chops.

PET TALES By Rachel Gies

Then they'd jump on one of the huge round picnic tables to receive their evening vittles. This went on each and everyday for months. It didn't matter if Jesse came home at three in the afternoon or midnight, the cats would be waiting and at times, Jesse swore they were smiling at him. Even in the coldest months of winter, the cats waited for their meals. Jesse had made a comfortable area with some old blankets inside the shed behind the house.

Months passed and all seemed great! Max and Karl finally gained some weight and had even grown slightly fat, or so it seemed. Max looked just a bit larger than Karl. For some time, even though Max was the smaller of the two he seemed to have gained weight more rapidly. Maybe he ate more than Karl? Soon, Max started acting strange and wouldn't come out for his nightly meals. He remained inside the shed lying on his blanket. Jesse and Shelly became concerned and wondered if he might be sick. Maybe he ate a mouse that was spoiled or had gotten into some food that might have been poisoned. Rumor had it that several animals around the area had been poisoned. Jesse decided to take the cat to the vet.

He wasn't sure at first if Max would even allow him to pick him up. Jesse had been able to get close enough, but he never attempted picking them up because of his severe allergies. He usually kept a slight distance between himself and the cats. He knelt down by Max and in a soothing voice told the feline he would take him to the vet so that he could get him the help he needed. Suddenly, as Jesse reached out Max showed his claws and hissed. Never before in all these months had either one of the cats hissed at Jesse or Shelly.

Ellie

Jesse realized something must be terribly wrong and he continued talking to the cat in soft tones. Afraid that the cat might be hurt Jesse put his own well being aside. As he made another move toward the cat, Jesse saw the why Max was so defensive. Jesse looked closer at something small and furry beneath Max that was moving! KITTENS!? Half a dozen tiny little fluffy kittens! Max was in actuality Maxine! Jesse now understood why Max was hissing at him and backed off. Maxine was only trying to protect her babies. Jesse was pleasantly surprised as he watched the adorable kittens snuggle close to Max...Maxine. Everyone figures Karl was the father because they were always together and they made such good parents. He would help Maxine keep a watch over the kittens while she went to the picnic table for her dinner. Then when Maxine finished, she would return to where her kittens were waiting and then it was Karl's turn to eat.

With the tender loving care given by Jesse and Shelly and the two cats the kittens quickly became full grown cats. There were only four of the kittens left from the original litter because one died shortly after birth and another one disappeared. No one was sure if the tiny critter had just wandered off too far or had become a snack for some wild animal.

Years passed and Jesse and Shelly still enjoy their little "zoo" of kittens. There must be at least thirty to fifty cats roaming the backyard. No one has kept count. Many others have joined the pack since Maxine and Karl and are enjoying a carefree lifestyle. All continue waiting for Jesse each and everyday. As soon as they hear his car pull up the driveway there's mayhem among the wild. Like herds of cattle, the cats come charging out from every tree or bush. Jesse even makes arrangements for someone to feed the cats if he's gone for a few days.

Jesse's got a running tab at the vet's office because some of the cats go into a war zone and fight over whose turf they are on. Some get injured

PET TALES By Rachel Gies

from a fight with another animal that doesn't belong there. Many come home limping and meowing after their battles have been fought. Jesse has found some cats with their ears ripped and others with a broken leg or worse, missing an eye. Bloodied and battered these cats have crawled back into the yard and Jesse would reach out and gather the injured and take them to the vet if he is unable to treat the animal himself. One would be shocked to see their veterinarian bills. But I know that Jesse doesn't care about that. To him and to Shelly the animals are worth the cost.

    I suppose I am not surprised. After all, I've know him my whole life, he's my little brother. He'd always bring home stray or injured animals and then try talking our parents into keeping them. Jesse never wavered in his compassion for nature's creatures, even though he spent half of his life at the doctor's office going through all kinds of allergy tests. By the way, Jesse recently inherited Henry, a ten year old dog, completely deaf, going blind and has diabetes. Henry's previous owner passed away and knowing how Jessie loved animals requested for Henry to be taken care of by Jesse and left him quit a bit of money in her Will. She knew Jessie would take good care of Henry and the town's strays. ✱

Chapter 22

BUNNIES IN THE BASEMENT

It all began 7 years ago on a Memorial Day. Robyn and her husband, Andy, decided to do some work in their garden. It was a cool morning and Robyn, Andy and their son Reece, had just finished a delicious lunch. They enjoyed quality family time working together in their yard. Andy and Reece had already gone outside while Robyn cleaned up the dishes. Andy started working on the landscaping and Reece, who was just 4 years old, wanted to help his parents. Like most kids, Reece loved digging in the dirt and within minutes he was scooping up mud and filling his small bucket.

When Robyn finished in the kitchen she joined her boys in the yard. Both Andy and Robyn worked diligently for a while when suddenly, they heard Reece calling out, "Bunnies, baby bunnies!" Robyn and Andy raced over to where Reece was sitting pointing his little hand at something on the ground. To their amazement he showed them a small hole where inside several baby bunnies huddled together! Gently, Andy, who was wearing his garden gloves, lifted out two of the tiniest wild rabbits. They were so tiny and looked like little mice!

Now, we all know that there's nothing more precious than a newborn baby bunny. They couldn't have been more than a few days old and the thought of leaving these poor little creatures out there to die, or have them possibly devoured by some wild animal roaming around was more than the family could bear. Gently, Andy carried the bunnies inside the house and

PET TALES By Rachel Gies

down to the basement. They were put into a wicker basket on top of a fluffy towel. Robyn looked on the internet for some information about caring for wild rabbits. She was worried that the bunnies without their mother might not survive. She learned a bunny mom would leave her babies and not return if handled by a human. So they knew that keeping them inside and comfortable was their best option at this point. Reece loved those little bunnies.

A couple of days later, while Robyn was at work, Reece had the babysitter call his mother. He was screaming, "Mommy, the bunnies are dead!" Robyn felt so bad thinking how traumatic it is for a child to lose a pet. She decided to get Reece a bunny for his 5th birthday. At the pet store Reece picked out a small dwarf black male bunny that was about 3 weeks old. Reece was overjoyed with his new best friend. They named him Nike and he quickly became an important member of the family along with their Standard Poodle named Jazz.

Nike was already litter trained and they kept a small cat bed on the center island in the kitchen for him. He had the run of the backyard and the house and would let the family walk right over and pick him up. He loved the family and his new home.

After 5 years living in the desert of New Mexico, the family moved to Illinois. Within a few months they decided to add yet another member to their family and adopted a cat named Sasha. Oh, it was hilarious to see the kitten and the bunny sharing the cat bed and hopping around the kitchen island. It was as if these two were brother and sister and didn't have a care in the world. Nike had the run of the main floor. One day when the kids were off from school, Reece and Robyn went to a local pet shop to get some food for Nike, Sasha and Jazz. Reece just had to see all of the animals.

He could literally spend hours there. As they walked up and down the aisles they giggled and pointed at all of the cute little bunnies.

Robyn stopped at a large lop eared rabbit. Sadly, this one had been badly abused and had lost half of his fur. It looked so pathetic Robyn's heart went out to the poor animal. It had been there for months and no one seemed to want it. Robyn looked at her son and she knew what she needed to do. There was no way they were going to walk away from this little fellow. Robyn paid just $10, for the bunny, probably because the owner of the pet shop was happy to get rid of this dismal looking creature. She knew they would give him a good home but she also knew better than to ask her husband about expanding the family. Of course he definitely would say, "No!". This was a "better to ask forgiveness than permission" situation.

So Robyn and Reece brought their new adopted friend, who they named Smudge, home despite what Andy would say. He threatened to feed them rabbit stew if they didn't return it! Robyn knew Andy wasn't serious, at least she hoped. Once again Robyn went on-line hoping to learn as much as she could about caring for this injured rabbit. She also wanted to know how to introduce the male rabbits to each other. The article recommended that they be kept separate, however; from the very start they seemed to like each other. Nike was always following Smudge around wherever he went. They became best buddies. Nike was so happy to have a new friend that he just couldn't get enough of Smudge. Robyn moved both bunnies down to the basement.

It was such fun to watch all the animals playing with each other. Sasha stayed close

Bunnies in the Basement - Parker Saunders

PET TALES By Rachel Gies

by watching the bunnies while Jazz would just act protective of the trio.

They all seemed to grow and glow for a while, and spent many happy hours playing and chasing each other around. After about 3 months, Smudge started to lose his fur again, which worried Robyn. In the seven years that they had Nike, they never had to take him to the vet because he was such a healthy and active rabbit. She decided to take Smudge for a check-up. The vet informed her that the rabbit had mites! The vet gave Smudge injections to rid him of the little varmints.

Robyn also told the vet that Smudge did not seem to act the same as the other male which made her wonder if Smudge had been neutered. That's when the vet turned Smudge over on his back and smiled. To Robyn's astonishment, he, was a she, and was nesting. Oh, my. That was a real shocker for Robyn. No wonder, she thought, this was the reason Smudge seemed so different from the other rabbit. They were always snuggling and frolicking around. Robyn and the vet thought it best to have Nike neutered.

What a surprise it was when Robyn told Andy. That could have ended with more babies! No more mites and a neutered Nike. Everyone was happy (Nike not so much, maybe). What's next for the trio of furry friends and their protector: Nike, Smudge, Sasha ... *and ... aaaallll that ... Jazz!?*. ✱

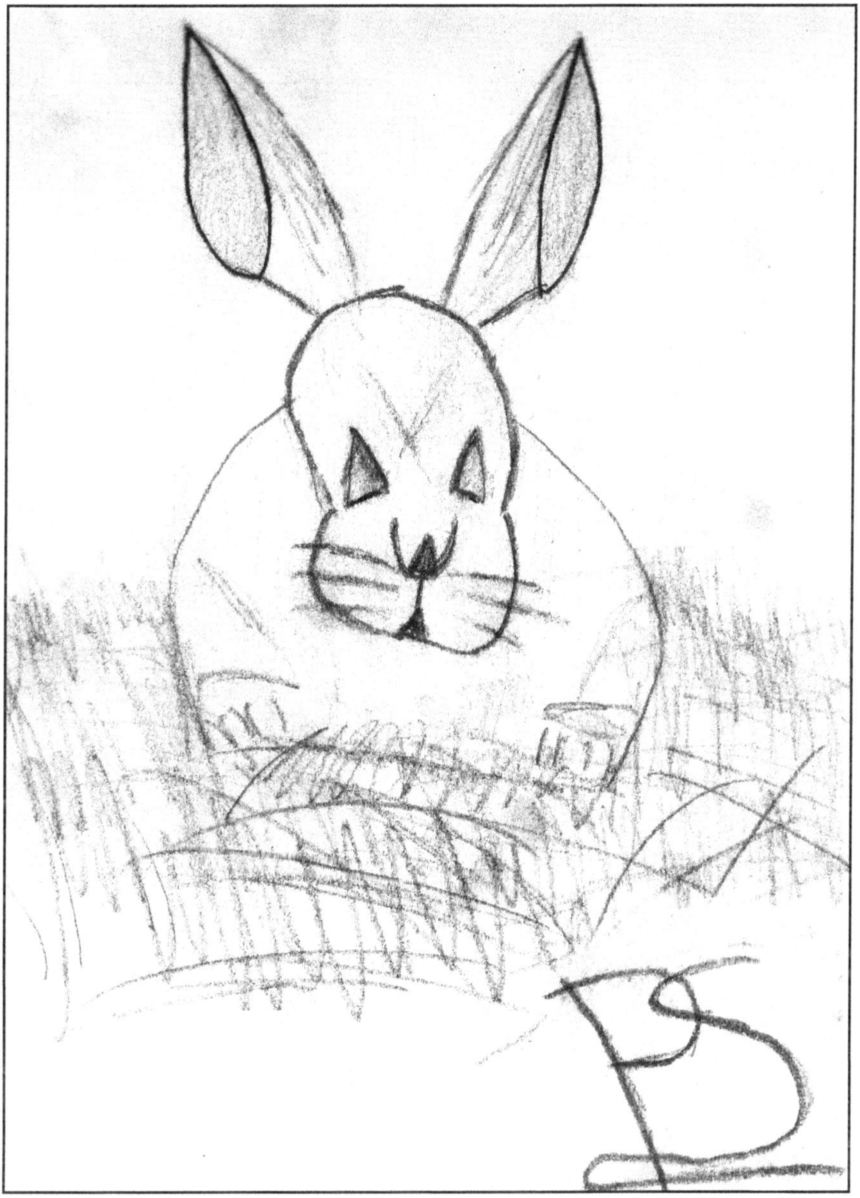

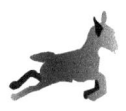

Lamari Hall

Chapter 23

AN UNEXPECTED FRIEND

In a small town called Fertile, near Grand Forks (where Minnesota and North Dakota almost meets up with Canada) Johnny (ten) and Joe (eight) spent some of the summer on their Uncle Jay's farm, just outside of town. Johnny enjoyed the busyness of the farm and they both helped with chores.

One day, Johnny and Joe were playing outside when they noticed an animal wandering towards them. It looked like a dog, resembling a German shepherd, but upon closer observation it was actually a wolf. Johnny didn't seem to be frightened at all. The poor thing looked hungry so Joe ran and grabbed some food leftover from dinner and Johnny threw it as close as he could to the wild animal. Hesitantly the wolf inched closer, looking cautiously at the boys and lapped up the food. It was kind of strange seeing a wolf in broad daylight this close to town. Johnny slowly walked towards the animal. Despite his mom's warning to be careful around stray dogs Johnny was getting closer than he should. He coaxed the animal toward him with a chicken leg. The wolf paced back and forth and jumped back as Johnny got closer.

This went on for several days. Each morning Johnny left food for the wolf that waited outside. Softly speaking to the wolf Johnny tried to earn his trust, wanting to pet him, but the animal refused to come into Johnny's reach. Each time Johnny lifted his hand to pet the animal it would run in circles around him. One day, the wolf actually allowed Johnny to touch his

PET TALES By Rachel Gies

fur and it wasn't long before the wolf started to follow him everywhere.

When Johnny went off to the Sand Hill River for a swim the wolf followed him and patiently waited for his friend to come out and he'd escort him back to the house. Wherever Johnny went the wolf followed him like a puppy. His little brother Joe wanted to make friends with it too Johnny wouldn't let him for his own safety. The relationship between the two became an experience Johnny would never forget.

Sadly, all good things come to an end and one day the wolf didn't return for his morning meal. Johnny watched over his shoulder for the wolf all day. Days passed without him. Johnny began to realize that the wolf wasn't coming back.

Johnny went back to the farm for a visit that fall with Joe and Dad. Uncle Jay mentioned the trouble he'd had with some "dawg-gone wolves". A while back he'd lost his heard to a wild wolf pack. He said that he finally managed to shoot a number of them and since then the killing of his sheep had stopped.

I'm sure you guessed like Johnny did what happened to his little wolf pal. Being a young boy of ten Johnny cried for his lost buddy but also understood that wolves aren't meant to be pets and he probably shouldn't have encouraged it to hang around his uncle's farm. Though he missed the animal he knew in his heart that his uncle was right. Every so often Johnny thinks back on that special bond and he has shared the tale with warning his children and now his grandchildren. ✱

Chapter 24

A FLY IN THE CAT BOX

Why ... in the middle of winter ... is a persistent pesky little fly zooming around my head, spiraling through the rooms and driving me absolutely batty? The problem is the evasiveness of the pest as it flies non-stop, dive bombs my head making it impossible to catch. Weapon in hand I'm ready to go after the enemy and end this miserable little beast—but now it won't land. Now it's flying around the cat's litter box! SO GROSS!

I just didn't expect to have any flies inside the house at this time of year. I thought flies died during the cold weather, or were in hibernation some place during the winter months. Obviously I was wrong because this character had been giving me the run around all day.

The fiasco began earlier when I took my dog for his usual walk. It was a cold crispy day and when we got done shivering outside, we came back in to warm up. Low and behold, without any warning and so suddenly, there was this humongous thing buzzing around the laundry room like a small helicopter. At first it looked like an "unidentified flying object", but then I realized this UFO was in actuality a yucky fly.

As if we didn't have enough trouble during the summer from all of the insects inside the house! We had finally gotten rid of all the wasps that had invaded our home and terrorized us for years. They had set up camp inside the walls the last three summers. They spent all winter multiplying inside those walls and came out during the spring. I was told by the pest

PET TALES By Rachel Gies

control company, that they like making their nests during the fall and sleep soundly during the winter. All summer long they lived with us rent free! Oh what joy having to duck from those ugly little beasts as they attacked us—stingers prepped and ready! We sprayed so much pesticide we were still dizzy from the fumes.

This clever little fly was not just surviving, it was trying to drive me crazy. It was as if he knew what I was up to. I just couldn't seem to get him to land so that I could finish him off. I got out the bug killer and it seemed as if he stopped momentarily to consider his defensive. There was no doubt in my mind that he knew my next move. I also found an old reliable fly swatter so I could move in double fisted. I prepared myself physically and mentally for the biggest battle yet. I was ready to ambush him when suddenly he was gone. All was quiet and as far as I could see there was no fly.

I just knew that he was hiding somewhere watching me. He knew it was war and we were enemies. I could feel his micro-mini eyes staring but that could be my over active imagination. I've been stalked by hundreds of wasps over the last three summers and my insect instincts were fine tuned. I might be just a little paranoid and cautious. I decided to bide my time and out wait him. After all, he wasn't going anywhere and I knew he had a weakness: The cat box.

I planned for my next strategy as I pretended being busy doing something else to keep my mind off my opponent. Maybe he'd just go away or drown in the cat litter. Wishful thinking? Perhaps. I waited another couple of hours and then I snuck back into the laundry room where I knew he'd be busy. Yup! He was still circling the cat box as if on a mission. At least he remained in one room making it easier for me to attack him.

I don't like using insect spray inside because of my pets but for this guy I'd make an exception. Once again, I made my attempt to go after the "flying Dutchman" and bring him down. I had given him a pet name because the more time I spent with him the more I started feeling some compassion for him. Maybe respect is a better word. As I continued to watch him go another couple of rounds then hide, I wondered if he'd ever tucker out and just give up. Do flies ever take a nap? He never seemed to settle down and me a chance to swat at him.

This fly reminded me about an old movie I saw years ago called "The Fly." I think the original movie had Vincent Price in it and was made in 1958, about a scientist named Andre Delambre who becomes obsessed with his latest creation, a matter transporter. He has varying degrees of success with it and eventually decides to use a human subject, himself, with tragic consequences. During the transference, his DNA become merged with a fly's DNA, which was accidentally shut in the machine with him. He winds up with the fly's head and one of its arms while the fly winds up with Andre's head and arm. I had nightmares from that movie for quite a while.

I actually started to admire the little creature for his stamina and strength to go on. He managed to keep me at bay for hours! He seemed to know when I was ready to strike and knew how to evade my swat. I not only admired the pest, I started to feel sorry for it. I started to feel ashamed and wondered if I should just let it be. How long was a fly's life expectancy living in this environment anyway? Isn't a fly's life short lived? He couldn't live too much longer during the winter could he? I believed that this fly must have sensed my reluctance to kill. He actually slowed down his pace and landed quietly on top of the cat litter. As I stood in silence, holding my breath, I knew what had to be done. Letting this poor tired thing sit

PET TALES By Rachel Gies

there and rest was agonizing for me to watch. I could almost hear his tiny lungs heaving with relief as he rested. It was as if he had fallen asleep. He certainly looked peaceful parked atop the kitty pile. Slowly, without taking a breath I raised my hand that held the fly swatter. I knew I had to act now before he awoke and continued the chase. Then before I realized what had happened there was a loud ka-boom! Without too much bother, down came my swatter. The little guy probably never knew what hit him. And the fly flew no more. I eased my grip on my weapon I knew that the fly was no longer on top of the cat litter. He was in the litter buried deep and I believe that at last he had found peace. ✻

Chapter 25

PAMPERED PETS

A pet becomes a member of the family and we treat them as such by spoiling them with toys, blankets, beds, fancy clothes and then some. We even pick up items for ourselves such as socks, key chains, bumper stickers and t-shirts. But our pets don't notice if they have diamond collar or a plain one. My dog would eat anything tossed into the air and he drank from the toilet. And when the kids tried dressing him up he'd be so insulted he'd tear it off faster than they could put it on.

I have a friend who has three cats and she spoils them rotten. Her house is taken over with tons of toys and each cat has its own mini kitty house. She has two boy cats and one girl cat who is the QUEEN! Guess who's in charge? All three cats have their claws and you should see the furniture. What's so weird is that when we visit she demands we take off our shoes!

I can tell you I was attached to all my animals but some of the things people do is going a bit too far. I think what pets really need is love, food, some gentle pets, medical care when necessary and a safe place to call home. They don't need fancy dishes and clothes.

Everyone does what they can for their beloved pets and hopefully, what they can afford. We all want a happy healthy pet and as long as we understand the important part of having a pet is giving them a loving home and taking good care of their needs in return we will be adored and protected everyday they are with us.

PET TALES By Rachel Gies

My friend Gail has a small dog, as cute as a button, she could be a Maltese. This dog is adorable in every way. She's as tiny as a toy poodle and as fluffy and cuddly as a bunny. Gail adores her dog and treats this pup as if it were human; *or should I say more like a spoiled child.* The dog's name is Pebbles. Gail brings Pebbles to work with her every day. It's a good thing she owns her own beauty salon. Working anywhere else would not allow a dog running around the office.

Little Pebbles has her own wardrobe which consists of, I kid you not, fancy dresses and pant outfits in hot pink, fuchsia, gold, silver and lilac. She has her own little built-in closet. She even has her own jewelry engraved with her name or initials. Believe it or not, Pebbles also owns a few matching purses. Then there are doggy shoes and goulashes for when the weather is bad.

When Gail flies anywhere, she brings Pebbles along inside her designer travel bag. She slides the cushy bag under her seat during the flight. Pebbles is finicky when it comes to the food she eats from her monogrammed dishes and those dishes are more expensive than any piece of china I've ever owned.

There are so many lonely people in the world who could only dream of being loved like Pebbles. Gail never had children and I think the little pup is filling that void. Once every six weeks, Gail takes her to a doggy spa where she receives treatments fit for a queen. Also, since Gail is in the beauty business, Pebbles gets hair treatments to keep her coat shiny and fluffy.

I wonder if there's anyone out there who takes their kitten everywhere? But cats seem to like it better at home and don't enjoy car rides or people as much as dogs do. ✶

Naomi

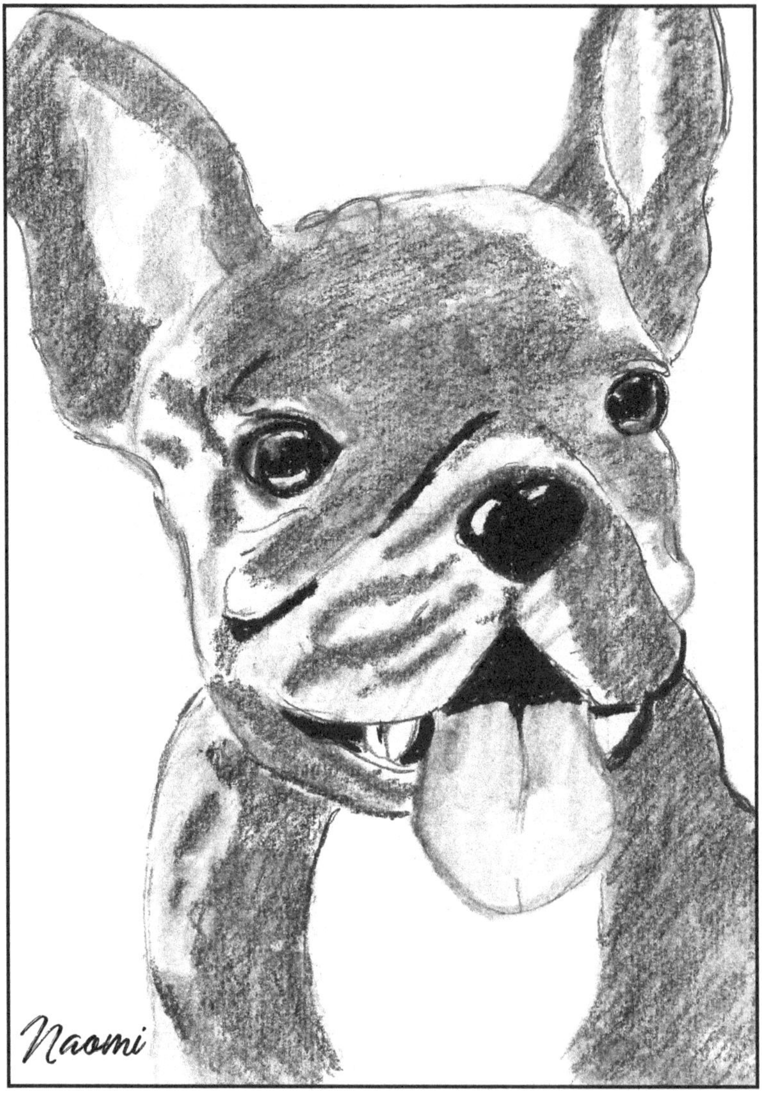
Naomi

Chapter 26

COCO AND CHANEL

People love their animal companions. House pets can be considered loyal friends and keep you company while you treat them well and care of them. They love the entire family but may feel a closer bond to the one who feeds them.

Here's my favorite story about my friend's daughter, Anna. Anna loved walking and taking care of her two dogs; Coco and Chanel. Coco was the male and Chanel was the female and they both adored Anna and would follow her everywhere she went. Why, you ask, would she name her dogs after a designer? Well, Anna loved fashion design and she wanted more than anything to be a fashion designer. She also had a bird she named Karl who was also named after a designer.

When Anna was eighteen she couldn't afford to attend college to become a designer. She realized she needed a job to support herself because her parents couldn't afford to pay for her college and school for her two other siblings. She looked for a job as close as she could get to the fashion world, retail. Not only was Anna talented she was also tall and very attractive and had a great eye when helping people put the right pieces together.

She enrolled in college once she received financial aid. Her teachers loved everything she created and soon Anna became well known in the area. Anna was also instrumental in promoting the store's clothing by

PET TALES By Rachel Gies

modeling her original designs and before long she finished school and opened her own boutique. Anna's boutique was busier than she'd imagined and she hired several young people right away.

Anna soon became well known and created the most beautiful styles inspired by well known designers. She created such beautiful copies of famous fashions the people would fly in just to get her designs. Then she met Pierre, a man who had heard about her designs and offered her a huge opportunity to come work for him in France. She explained that she needed time to think about it because she knew if she left the country her pets Coco and Chanel wouldn't survive without her. You see Coco and Chanel weren't so young anymore and Anna was afraid something bad would happen to her beloved pets. Eventually, she declined the offer and stayed in her own boutique. A few weeks later she received a call from the same man with another offer she couldn't refuse. He offered to purchase her designs and bring them to life in France.

Coco and Chanel still thought her world revolved around them because Anna brought them with her almost every day unless they went to a play date or doggy daycare where they met and played with other dogs until Anna picked them up.

Yes, it was a great time for all and a profitable journey for Anna. Then she ran into Pierre, the man from France that helped her to become successful by promoting and advertising her in his homeland. Pierre asked her to dinner and afterward, dancing. As one thing led to another they fell madly in love and soon talked about marriage. Now as I told you, Pierre lived in France and Anna didn't want to go there because of her fear for Coco and Chanel. Pierre tried to understand but was saddened by Anna's refusal to go to France with him. Eventually, this became a big issue. Anna couldn't leave her pets and eventually broke off the relationship.

Today, Anna is in her late 80s and has retired after selling her boutique and designs to Pierre's oldest son Andre who continues selling Anna's beautiful fashions to people around the world. ✶

Chapter 27

MOUSE CATCHERS

    As I was cleaning the patio doors I noticed a beautiful cat in my yard sitting there just looking around. It seemed as if he was waiting for something to show up. It was getting colder and fall was on the way. Most trees seemed to be losing their leaves fast but they fell slowly and methodically on the dry grassy ground and blew around the yard. As I stood there quietly watching this cat I realized he was ready to spring into when whatever he was waiting for showed up. Now, this isn't the first cat to visit my yard. We have at least three more that come around pretty often and boldly walk up onto the deck to peek inside the house through the sliding door hoping for scraps of food maybe. I would love to bring them inside because my love for animals is so great and whenever I see any stray animal I want to take it in and care for it. But I know who these visitors belong to and their owners love them as much as I do. What I love most is watching the cats hang out on the deck and share their great hunting skills.

    Cats seem to have great patience because they spend so much time sitting very still like a statue until a critter strolls by, unaware. The moment between the statue like stillness and the spotting of the mouse is awesome because the cats shift into gear ready for what is usually a very short chase. Luckily these cats come back almost every day and we've had very few visitors from the rodent family in our basement. It sure saves on mouse traps. They are the best neighborhood watch, ever.

Our old cat Morris was a feisty creature and thought he owned the jungle. Every cat in the neighborhood was afraid of Morris and knew he was in charge except he had only one fear: mice. Morris was afraid of mice and when a mouse was spotted that cat would leap from wherever he was and run off and hide. He was the biggest coward when it came to mice. In fact, we had to set traps to catch mice because Morris refused.

When Daphne, the next door neighbor's cat met up with Morris there was be a hissing contest that lasted until both beasts ran out of breath. Daphne absolutely hated Morris with a passion until one day something happened that united the two forever. Daphne happened to prance by while Morris was lying on the concrete steps basking in the sun. Suddenly Biff, the terrier from across the street (the neighborhood canine bully) flew after Daphne and caught her before she could reach a tree. Biff clamped his teeth on the poor girl's tail and the entire neighborhood heard Daphne screeching.

Morris awoke, saw what was happening and ran to Daphne's rescue. He, who was so afraid of a tiny mouse, pounced on top of Biff and dug his claws into the dog's back until he released the poor feline. Watching the scene unfold before them, Daphne's owners gasped in horror, then sighed with relief once Morris saved their dear girl. Poor Daphne was pretty shaken but realized that Morris had come to her rescue.

Her attitude toward him changed and she allowed her hero to sit with her and share the neighborhood watch. Turns out they shared more than that! They also shared a small litter of adorable kittens. ✶

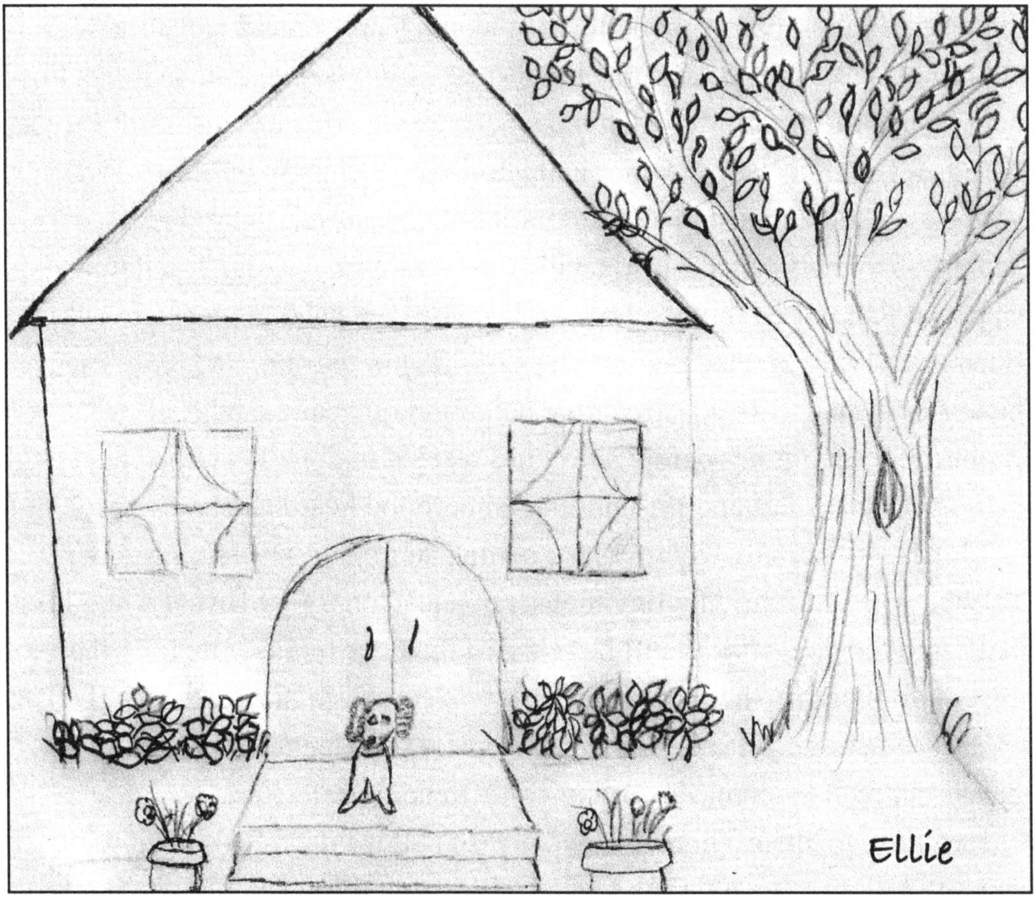
Ellie

Chapter 28

LOST AND FOUND

Most animals have great instincts and sense of direction like dogs and cats and when roaming free they can usually find their way home. Cats are often used to being free outside to roam the neighborhood so we expect them to always find their way back, but dogs tend to run after something and don't pay so much attention to everything around them and how far away from home they get.

A close friend of mine, Joe, had to move to a retirement home where animals weren't permitted. So, sadly he had to leave his dog, Chief, with his brother. But the good news was that he knew his brother's farm was a great place where his dog would be loved and treated well.

His brother brought Chief with when he helped Joe move into his new home, 14 miles from the farm. As Joe watched them drive away he felt lonely and sad wishing his buddy could stay with him.

Several days later when he returned from his walk he couldn't believe his eyes. There on the front step sat his dog with bleeding paws and matted fur, looking like a drowned rat. Of course he decided he would never leave his dog again and he begged the owner of his apartment to let the pet stay and after explaining what the dog had gone through the sympathetic owner agreed. It's truly amazing how his dog possessed such an uncanny instinct to find his way back to his beloved owner.

So, one wonders about other animals like cats that are independent

PET TALES By Rachel Gies

creatures, and many times act as if they don't care about their owners like dogs do. However, having had cats myself I know that while they may not be as affectionate as dogs, many of them adore their owners. I have even heard people say they believe animals communicate with each other.

Then I heard this story and what happened when a guy's cat ran away didn't return home for two days. Someone responding to the missing cat post on twitter. This stranger (in more ways than one) wrote that she spoke with other cats in the neighborhood when her cat disappeared. She asked the neighborhood cats, 'If you see my cat, please tell her to come home'. The missing cat's owner had nothing to lose so he gave it a try. He went around town looking for cats to talk to. The following morning his cat was at the front door. Um ... seriously?

Of course we're all skeptical of such stories, especially when someone posts it on twitter. Most of us would say it was a coincidence and there could be a number of reasons and explanations as to why the cat returned home. However, it was surprising to see the number of responses from others who said they had similar results with their own lost pets after speaking to stray animals in the area. It does make one pause and wonder if this method might actually work or were this many people batty?

It's nice to think that it may work ... Sure, people will think you've lost it—but if it works, we really don't care what others think. Animals surprise us every day and they are probably smarter than we give them credit for. So next time a beloved pet is lost, look for stray cats and ask the squirrels. They might just help you out. Think of *Dr. Doolittle* or *Lady and the Tramp*! ✷

Chapter 29

DEAR LITTLE FELLA

WARNING! SAD ALERT: This is a letter from my broken heart to my dearest little Chuckie. I am sharing this because kids don't always see what adults go through when we lose a pet. It hurts for all of us.

My Dearest Little Chuckie,

It's been a few months since you've gone, yet I feel the deep loss as if it was yesterday. You were always by my side when I needed you. The day I buried my loved one you were there for me when friends and family left. So many times when I cried myself to sleep you cuddled up with me as if you knew how much pain I felt. I believe you felt the pain as well. You loved him and missed him too. I would sometimes wake up and feel your soft, silky, furry coat close to my cheek and hear the beat of your tiny heart ringing out. Oh, yes, tiny you were, but your love was huge and unconditional. You gave me courage to get up each day so that I could once again face another without the one I so dearly loved.

I was consumed with my loss but there you were nipping at my ankles as if trying to bring me back to reality, away from my grief. How many hours did you lay by the door just waiting for the garage to open? How much time did you spend alone waiting to be with me? Yet, there you always were, patiently waiting and eager to please as if I never left.

PET TALES By Rachel Gies

Never, ever, were you in a bad mood, you never complained or demanded of me. You gave me your trust and loyalty since the day we met.

You eagerly lapped up whatever food I put in front of you and I knew when you looked up at me, food stuck to your adorable whiskers that I fell in love with you all over again. With that twinkle in your eyes as you looked into mine I felt lucky having you in my life. You loved me unconditionally and you always seemed to know when I needed a cuddle.

When you got sick I think you sensed your imminent demise yet I never realized how sick you were. I promised you that I was there for you and you seemed to understand. While trying to nurse you back to health my heart ached for you to get well even though I knew time was running out. I know you tried getting better for me, but it was your time. I think we both knew you couldn't live like that much longer. That was not the quality of life that you deserved. Even when I took you to the vet to care for you there was a determination inside you that fought hard to stay alive. When the vet told me you were a trooper we both knew deep down that no matter how hard you fought you just wouldn't get any better. I didn't want to leave you alone there because I was scared that when I returned you wouldn't be waiting for me. But it was time for you to leave me.

Once again my heart was broken but I found peace knowing you were no longer feeling pain. I took home the tiny urn protecting your ashes inside. I shall carefully lay you to rest in the yard you knew so well. Your precious memories will forever be in my heart and one day when I leave this earth I know we will be together again and there will be no pain.

Thank you for choosing me. Thank you for blessing my life.

I love you my little fella. ✻

Chapter 30

THE GIFT

Cheri and her husband Max were still getting over the loss of their dog Romeo. Their friends, Robyn and Andy, decided what they needed was a new puppy and they found the perfect one for them from the Humane Society. Now most people know better and would always check with their friends before gifting a pet. But they saw how unhappy they were and they thought that Cheri and Max would love having another puppy to cheer them up (they were such good dog parents). In memory of Romeo they named the new puppy Juliet.

Max was visiting his parents in Italy. Cheri wasn't sure that he would be too thrilled about another puppy so soon. After all, he wouldn't come close to their beloved Romeo and puppies need a lot of attention. Plus they couldn't take another heartbreak. Max had not completely recovered from losing Romeo.

Now, it wasn't that Max didn't like animals, he loved them, but Max was getting close to retirement and he and Cheri had planned on doing some traveling. The first thing they wanted to do was take a cruise around the world. That would certainly make having a puppy impossible. It was a definitely too soon.

Rather than asking them to return Juliet and to avoid any hurt feelings Cheri asked them to keep the pup at their house until Max came home.

PET TALES By Rachel Gies

They were sure that once Max met Juliet and saw her cuteness he would fall in love, again.

It was a good thing Cheri asked them to keep her for a while. Juliet had a behavior problem that surfaced. Maybe it was PADHD (Puppy Attention Deficit Hyperactivity Disorder) the friends tried everything to house-train her themselves.

Ellie

Even though they got her plenty of doggy toys to chew on Juliet tore up shoes, purses, blankets, you name it. When she ate medication when she was chewing on a purse she ran in circles and went into a seizure, foaming from her tiny mouth. Robyn grabbed her and drove her to the veterinarian. They had to pump her tummy of the medication. They all realized Juliet could have died and their love for her was overwhelming. Robyn and the family decided to take Juliet to a professional puppy trainer.

When Max finally returned, Cheri explained what their friends had done with the best of intentions and that Robyn's family was caring for the dog. That night, Cheri and Max went to meet Juliet. Juliet ran up to them and sat down with her two front paws in the air.

"Shake hands" Robyn commanded. Juliet lifted her tiny paw into Cheri's hand. Juliet behaved wonderfully and was very eager to please. Oh yes, Juliet is now a model puppy with great manners and a wonderful disposition. The obedience training had definitely paid off.

Cheri and Max realized how much the family loved Juliet and they wouldn't dream of taking her from Robyn's family.

Maybe one day Cheri and Max will think about adopting another puppy but until then they will enjoy the freedom of visiting Juliet and go home when they've had enough. Just like some grandparents do. ✷

Chapter 31

A GOATEE TALE

Written and Illustrated by: Aubrey Barbeau
11-Year-Old Student at the Chain Exploratory Center

Once upon a time there was a goat named Luna. Luna was always getting into trouble. She was always getting out and running all over the place. Luna was a huge trouble maker. She was possibly the most troublesome goat on earth.

One summer day she got out (which was a normal day for Luna). When I walked outside, there she was on the porch. I ran to catch her. She ran around the corner so I followed her and there she was in the back yard with all of my goats trailing behind her. It looked like a goat parade! I ran to get my Dad and my brother to help me wrangle the goats.

When we came back outside the goats were all over the place! They were scattered from the pond to the apple orchard and everywhere in between.

PET TALES By Rachel Gies

One after another we fenced them all in. It came down to the final goat, LUNA! We dove! We ran! We slid! We did everything we could but she was uncatchable! That was Luna!

We were tripping and diving at all four legs. Every time we dove, she jumped and we'd miss her by inches! On the final dive my brother finally snagged her back leg. I raced to grab Luna around her neck and slipped the lead over her head. My brother and I walked Luna back to the barn. Our dad smiled looking proud as we locked her safely in the pen. For now at least. ✸

Chapter 32

THE TALE OF FRED

Written by: Maggie Miller
9-Year-Old Student at the Chain Exploratory Center

Once upon a time, there was a girl named Alice. Alice had always wanted a pet, like most children. Sadly, there wasn't enough room in their tiny countryside home.

"Please, Mother, I'd do anything! I don't care if I even get a raccoon! Please, Mother, please!" Alice begged.

"No, Alice, I've told you so many times! NO!"

Alice couldn't stop thinking about the pet that isn't hers. Every night she dreamed about getting a pet, taking care of it, playing with it all day. She knew that that couldn't happen. Until the next day…

That morning, Alice woke up with a sense of curiosity. She wandered into the forest, without even bothering to change out of her pajamas. She strode through the leaves and trees.

Pit pat … Pit pat … pit pat …

Alice heard the noise as she stepped around prickly raspberry bushes. "Got 'em!"

Sitting there, was a gray, fluffy possum. She'd been searching all day and finally, right in front of her—her new pet! Alice attempted to grab the possum, but failed. She decided to try again the next day.

She woke up hopeful. She decided that today was the day. She once again went into the forest. She walked around for hours, until she heard the familiar noise.

PET TALES By Rachel Gies

Pit pat... pit pat pit pat...

"Ah ha!" And there it was, clawing at her nightgown. An opossum. Alice's eyes filled with joy.

"Mother, Father!" she screamed bringing the opossum inside the house. "I found something!"

"So that's what you've been doing out there!" father says pitifully. "Now put it back, that thing is disgusting!"

Alice was devastated. "No, father! It is my pet!"

"Listen to your father." mother says.

"We can give it a bath, take it to the vet, and buy it the things it needs!"

"And why would we do that?" says father.

"Because I want him as my pet!" Alice shouts.

The family ends up keeping the opossum, and takes it to the vet.

"What should we name him?" mother asks.

"Fred." Alice confirms.

And they lived happily ever after.

THE END *

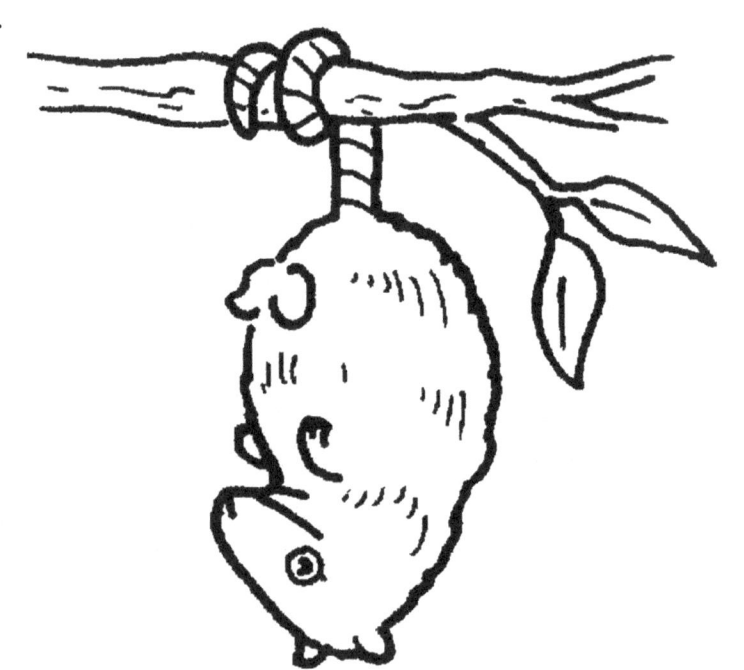

SECRET SERVICE HEALTHY STEALHY PET TREATS

The Wisconsin Secret Service started making pet treats for dogs and cats for the Waupaca Humane Society to sell and share. Their treats became Valentines for pets every year that kids could purchase for their pet. They donated the proceeds to the Humane Society. Pets love 'em and they're good for them too! You could cook without the supplements and they'll be loved just as much. You could just bake liver and your pet would love it too (they're gluten free)!

1 lb liver (boiled and purreed) or can of pumpkin
(If your pet has a beef allergy use lamb)
1/2 C olive oil
2 eggs

Google Quercetin Dihydrate, Collagen, and Brewers Yeast, Magnesium and Turmeric to see how good it all is for humans and dogs.

Dry Ingredients.
3 C Oat Flour (or more)
1 T Tapioca Starch
1 T Baking Powder
1 T Baking Soda
1 T Vitamin C
1 T Quercetin Dihydrate
1 T Collagen
3 T Brewers Yeast
1 T Magnesium Powder
2 T Turmeric
(You can use the first four ingredients and be just fine)

Boil the liver. When cooled blend with wet ingredients in Cuisinart until smooth (adding water from pot to blend if two dry). You can use a large can of 100% pure pumpkin instead. In one large bowl add dry ingredients.

Mix then knead like a firm clay. Add water a little at a time, if you add too much, add a little more oat flour. Form dough into a cube and cut into small cubes or roll into a snake and cut discs.

These come out super crunchy baked at 375° for 1 hour in a convection oven or longer until they are hard and dry in any other oven. Can freeze for another day. Vitamin C helps give the treats a longer shelf life. You can expect these treats to be good for 5-6 weeks in the fridge but you can keep them in the freezer forever. Your pet won't mind frozen treats! ✱

We LOVE our pets!!!